A ROARING, WHIMSICAL ADVENTURE

THE SYMBIGATE

SEAN M. T. SHANAHAN

FIRST EDITION

www.seanmts.com

Edited by the Ebook Launch Team.
Cover design and formatting by Miblart.

CHAPTER 1

Thomas Marrow

The moon was cast across the sky in crumbled ruin, trailing celestial wisps of pale green luminance as it arched over the lip of the ocean. The shattered celestial corpse dimmed as the sun rose over still waters, gorgeous, and completely lost on the figure standing at the base of the cliff.

He was tall with a broad chest, tanned olive skin, and dark hair. He wore a red frock coat, with bulky copper contraptions on his forearms, a cutlass strapped on the right hip, and a long knife on the left. He would have looked intimidating if he were not nervously fretting at the moment.

"Okay, okay, deep breath." Thomas rested his head on the smooth cliff face, lulled into false calm by the lapping waters. "You've got this."

After a few more deep breaths, Thomas opened his eyes and gazed upwards.

That was a mistake.

The sheer cliff loomed to challenge the celestial heavens. The surface grew craggy a dozen feet up, and the base smoothed from a time when the moon could affect the tide so drastically. The rough surface was gilded by the kindling embers of the sun as it crawled higher over the horizon. It cast the shadowy recesses into acute, hellish darkness, looking like the gnashing of teeth of some deranged demon.

"This cliff is insane." As dizziness took him, his foot slipped off the rocky edge and plunged into the ocean. "Cogrust!" He shook his foot in a useless attempt to rid himself of the chilling dampness. "Okay, enough of this, time to get to work."

He ran his hand nervously through his short dark hair and craned his neck again. The shattered moon still fought a losing battle against daylight, shining with green luminescence against the violet of a dying night. *At least that looks pretty, he* thought, raising his arms.

He flexed the symbioid woven into the bronze contraptions strapped to his forearms, triggering the latch. Grappling hooks launched from each arm, shooting into the air and embedding in the cragged rocky surface. He flexed the symbioid again, and the spool mechanism retracted the tethers, pulling him up the cliff face.

"Deep breath," he said again, his stomach dropping as he ascended. "Your equipment won't fail, your symbioid won't fail."

He reached the grapple point, and his ascent stalled. He flexed the symbioid again, and one of the hooks released from the wall. Hanging from one arm, Thomas swung back and accidentally glanced downwards.

"Oh ..." he said, feeling nauseous. "Just don't think about it."

Alternating his ascent between the different grapple hooks in his arms, he slowly made his way up the vertical surface. The moon debris orbited around the world and faded from view as the sun breached dawn and sailed into morning, lighting the ocean with red fire before it glistened like a sapphire.

"Just think on the mission."

Thomas Marrow was a Hired Hero, belonging to a group of questionably skilled mercenaries employed by municipalities or the wealthy to take on necessary but dangerous tasks.

And here he was fretting, *again*.

To him, it was a job to pay the bills while working for the good guys, or the closest to good you could get in this line of work. And occasionally, they did pro bono work for the little ones, which is the only reason Thomas had stayed on.

Today was not one of those jobs.

Recently a crime ring in the region had taken to abducting the children of the rich and ransoming them off for an insane cube colour. They made a killing—but this time, they screwed up. Their target was a high-end tailor, and they broke into his home while they were hosting the daughter of nobility.

They took the wrong girl by mistake, and Hired Heroes was employed to get the young princess back ... or was she a duchess? Or a baroness? It didn't matter. Thomas had tracked them to this stronghold, ruins on the edge of a sparsely inhabited island off the coast of Weznin. And he was going to get her back.

It was midmorning by the time Thomas reached the top of the cliffs. He was panting, and sweat soaked his deep maroon frock coat even as it billowed in the wind. With one last grapple he was over the lip of the cliff, quickly slinking behind the crumbling wall of the ruins. He took a moment to catch his breath and reconnoitre the situation.

The ruin was an old fortification facing out to sea, an imposing first line of defence against invaders in eons past. Now it was in shambles. It looked as though a meteor had hit it.

Something far more devastating than a meteor, Thomas thought.

Not one wall was fully intact, and the interior of the fortification was littered with a mess of boulders, collapsed walls, and precariously half-hanging rafters. There was a vague sense of rooms and battlements with somewhat intact stairs, and most of the roof had caved in with a large, greenish, foreign stone protruding through it. On the far side, there was a staircase, which was half obscured by a partition.

The ruined space within was littered with shards of red and gold, a sign of wealth from a time before the cataclysm. The sun poured through the voided windows and crumbling holes, reflecting off the shattered stained glass amongst the old debris, and cast an eerie, disjointed red-gold glow against the garish moon rock meteoroid.

Within the area there were several men playing cards, betting meagre-coloured cubes of white, violet, and indigo while bantering and laughing boisterously on occasion. Some blunderbusses lay across boulders nearby, but the majority of them had cutlasses or sabres.

There must be a guard somewhere on the perimeter as well, Thomas thought. *And someone with the baroness … duchess?*

"You'll eat what you're given, and you'll like it, you prissy girl!" A voice pierced the confines of the ruins and echoed off the many surfaces.

Thomas winced, but the men laughed as loud sobbing followed.

He homed in on the source of the voice. It came from the ruined staircase on the far side—shadows were cast against the wall by firelight on the first landing, depicting the image of a man stalking away from a hunched-over figure.

"Target acquired," Thomas whispered to himself.

He slinked into the ruins proper, taking advantage of the rocks and craggy boulders for cover while avoiding the shattered glass buried amongst the dust. The sounds of his passage were muffled by the echoing banter. Eventually, he wound his way around the giant, invasive moonstone in the centre of the room and found himself beneath the landing where he suspected that the duchess, baroness—where the hostage was being held.

He aimed a grapple upwards and waited. Not long after, the men erupted into laughter again, and Thomas shot his grappling hook into the landing above. Satisfied that no one heard his actions, he spooled himself upwards. Several metres off the ground, he swung back and forth—ignored the rising bile in his throat—caught the lip of the landing with his free hand, and pulled himself over slowly to find the captive sitting hunched against the wall.

She was a young girl, perhaps in her mid-teens, with pale skin and red puffy eyes. Her pink floor-length gown was filthy, and her blonde braided hair was strewn about in a mess. An uneaten bowl of stew sat before her.

Thomas's mouth began to salivate. *That smells amazing—why would she complain about that? Noble girls …*

Thomas crept silently up to her before she noticed him. She made a start, but he rushed in and forced his hand over her mouth while bringing his fingers to his lips.

"Don't fret," he said quietly, "I'm a Hired Hero. Your dad got me to come find you and bring you home."

Certain that she would not scream, he released her.

"Thank you," she sobbed.

"Shh," Thomas said, more to quiet her than to comfort her. "Let's get you out of here."

Before moving, Thomas had a thought. He scooped into the bowl of stew with the spoon and took a quick bite.

This is delicious! He regarded the hostage. *Noble girls …*

He moved her to the lip of the landing. Flexing his symbioid, he released the tether mechanism of his grapple and silently unspooled it. The symbioid ran along the tether like pale, sinewy tendons, contracting and moving like an extended limb. He wrapped the tether around her waist and pulled her tight. He quietly hooked his other grapple over the lip of the landing and lowered them both down onto ground level.

Getting the girl back to the lip of the cliff was easier than he had expected. The card players were still boisterous, which was ideal for sneaking. They quickly found themselves behind the weathered wall just a few feet from the cliff's edge.

"No," the girl said. "No, no, no, I can't go down that way."

"We have no choice … it's all open grassland on the other side of these ruins. They'd spot you in that dress a mile away."

"I can't do this!" she said, a little more loudly than Thomas would have liked. "I'm terrified of heights!"

"Shh," Thomas said and moved in close, putting reassuring hands on her shoulder, looking into her terrified eyes with his deep brown wells. "I'm afraid of heights too, terrified, but I have my grapples, and I'm gonna give you this."

He flapped open his maroon, calf-length coat, revealing his leather waistcoat with weaved-in bronze plates. He reached behind his back, pulled out a folded harness, and unfurled it. It was made from two tin plates with vents and corrugated tubes, and would fit over the shoulders via leather straps.

The backplate covered most of the upper back and had two nozzles poking outwards and down. He put the harness over the baffled girl and began tightening straps over her shoulders and under her arms as he explained what it was.

"This is an aero-break," he said. "There is a mechanical symbioid woven into the contraptions."

"Mechanical? As in dead? I don't want to weave with a symbioid, let alone a dead one! That's abhorrent!" she said, aghast.

Thomas rolled his eyes. "You won't have to weave with anything. It's woven solely into the contraption itself and doesn't require conscious control. It's purely mechanical, all automatic. Now as you fall …"

"You expect me to jump?!"

Thomas sighed. "No, this is just a precaution in case you fall while I am lowering you down. My grappling hooks take effort, you know? Now as you fall, the symbioid will siphon air through these vents and jettison it out the nozzles on the back. This will slow you down … understand?" He tightened the last of the straps.

"I … I think so."

"Good. Now don't worry, it's just a precaution. We won't have to use it, okay?"

She nodded timidly, and Thomas started unspooling his grapple tether to wrap around her when a voice shook him from his calm.

"THE DUCHESS IS MISSING!"

"Oh, so you *are* a duchess," Thomas said.

He peeked over the wall to check on the guard's reaction when his blood froze.

It was him. Golden cloak, scar across his right eye, he had aged, but it was him.

It was like Thomas was a thirteen-year-old kid again, cowering in his father's workshop with his eleven-year-old sister as battle raged outside. The memory echoed in every waking moment of his life. And now, one of the men he had been hunting for ten years was here, before him. The smell of burning wood, seared flesh, the rattling echo of trumpeted blunderbusses firing—splintering the door—and his sister shaking herself to pieces, shuddering with every shot. It all came rushing back.

He and Sybilla shrieked back when their father blinked and appeared in the room, covered in blood, panting, eyes wide with terror.

"I'm sorry!" he said. "I can't stop them, I'm sorry!"

The door burst inwards, filling the room with smoke as several men rushed in, knocking his father down and holding him in place. Then two men in golden cloaks waltzed in.

"So you really did embrace the tinkerer life, dear Barty? That is a shame, someone of your calibre reducing themselves to this," one of them said, pulling a golden round device from his cloak. "Why aren't you blinking away, I wonder? Is it the children hiding beneath that workbench? Or are you simply too exhausted from that fruitless battle? How's your heart, old chum?"

Barty remained stoic—if beleaguered—while staring down the gold cloak under the grip of two of the henchmen.

"Too tired to talk to your old friend, Barty?"

"Ringleader, you know nothing of friendship!" Barty spat.

The other gold cloak stepped in and smacked him across the face. "Better do it now," he said, "before he recovers enough to blink again."

"I don't think he'll be going anywhere with his offspring cowering nearby, Cain. But all right, I shan't delay," the ringleader said. He marched up to Barty and pressed the golden orb into his chest. He clicked a latch, and the orb sprung open, the embossed designs twisted with decorative gears as one of the hemispheres splayed open and dug into Barty's flesh. Barty screamed in agony as a bright light shone from the innards of the orb and the living symbioid was torn from Barty's flesh, siphoned from his body in thick tendrils and sucked into the orb, which clicked shut. "I'd wager you never really knew what you had woven with," the ringleader said, gazing at the orb in wonder.

"Now?" Cain asked.

"Now," the ringleader replied.

Cain plunged his knife into Barty's chest. His body went into spasms and then went limp.

Young Thomas screamed and rushed out from under the workbench and used his father's saw to slash at the murderer's face, tearing it down his eye. Cain screamed in fury and walloped Thomas across the face, knocking him out cold.

Young Thomas woke hours later beneath the burned-out remains of his father's workshop, his arms blistered and burned, but somehow, he survived. His sister Sybilla was nowhere to be found. He vowed that day that he would track down his sister and have revenge on the gold cloaks. He tinkered his own weapons from symbioid and bronze to make his grappling hooks and prepared to hunt the men who killed his family ever since.

He found no leads on the men until now, when the man who had plunged a knife into his father's heart stood over the ruins. His torn, scarred face glared down into the ancient wreckage, and Thomas was filled with long-lasting rage.

"Hero," the duchess said, "we must flee!"

Thomas took one look at her and side-kicked her off the cliff.

Her scream would have alerted the men to their whereabouts, but he was already charging in with his cutlass drawn, bellowing a battle roar.

Thomas cut down the first thug before he could react, then launched his grappling hook at the thug's companion before he could bring his blunderbuss around to fire. It hit him square in the chest, and he tumbled back into the ruins. With a whipping motion, Thomas retracted the grappling tether. He flexed the symbioid to curve the receding line and trip two other thugs from their feet as he slashed out at a third assailant, killing him with a blow to the neck.

Thomas flinched as the sentry from the outer wall clambered upon a boulder on the far side and peered through the sight of his blunderbuss.

The blast trumpeted from the tuba-like nozzle of the gun, and the shot pinged off a boulder nowhere near Thomas. The shooter began the frantic process of reloading. *Clumsy weapons,*

Thomas thought with a smile. He recovered from his flinch and finished the two tripped men before they could right themselves.

Another thug rushed him from the side and shoulder-charged him, causing him to drop his cutlass, and he shuffled back to create distance. He launched a grapple at the new assailant and flexed the tether to wrap around his neck, tightening it like a leash. The man grabbed at the tether with both hands, fighting against the choking line. Thomas drew his knife and roared; he retracted the tether, ripping the ensnared man towards him as he rammed his knife into his chest. He released the corpse and snatched up his fallen cutlass, wiping his knife on his coat before sheathing it.

The sentry with the blunderbuss appeared from between the boulders and fired point-blank, catching Thomas off guard. A glancing hit pinged off the bronze plating woven into his leather waistcoat.

Thomas glared at the bewildered man, who dropped his weapon and scrambled away through the boulders. Thomas did not pursue him—instead, he looked for his real target.

Cain.

His gaze darted around the ruins, searching, seeking, hunting for his prey. He grappled up onto a rock, brandishing his sword, and bellowed, "Cain! Where are you?!"

His question echoed off the walls into nothingness and was replaced by a different echo, the echo of slow applause. Thomas scanned the boulder-strewn area for the source of the noise, and his gaze was drawn upwards.

Cain was walking on the ceiling—his cloak hung awkwardly from his body—clapping slowly as he made his way over to Thomas.

Symbioid woven boots … Cogrust.

"I have to hand it to you," Cain said heartily, "even if they were a useless bunch of thugs, it is no easy feat to kill and scatter half a dozen men."

"There will be one more dead before the day is done, but you won't have a chance to flee like that last man," Thomas snarled.

"Now, what have I done to you to deserve such hostile attention?"

"My name is Thomas Marrow." Cain started; the sneer drained from his face. Thomas shot a grappling hook up to the ceiling and spooled upwards, hanging far above the jagged boulders and ruins below. He looked down, or—from his opponent's perspective—up into Cain's eyes. "You killed my father and took my sister."

"You can't be that little brat who did this to my face, can you?" Cain gestured to his scarred face as he drew his sword. "I thought we left you to burn in that little hovel of a workshop."

"I survived, and I have trained all my life to do what my father couldn't, to defeat you, to find my sister, and then to kill you all!"

Thomas attacked, ferociously, savagely. He fought with the burning need for vengeance that had fuelled him throughout all his training. He was the raging storm, but from the deftness with which his opponent parried his attacks, he may as well have been a gentle breeze.

Cain's symbioid boots gave him traction on the ceiling, and he could duck and weave around Thomas, who was secured solely to one point by his grapple, swinging wildly. Cain could also use both hands, while Thomas could only use one. Thomas was unused to fighting a man who was upside down, yet his quarry seemed to have much experience fighting from this vantage point.

After a furious but ineffective bout, Cain shifted back, preparing a riposte. Thomas glanced down at the ruins below. *My grapples would be of much better use against his boots amongst the rocky terrain.*

As Cain lunged forward to strike, Thomas rapidly unspooled his grapple and launched his second one against a low-hanging rafter, swinging away from the attack and landing heavily against the far wall. Thomas took the impact with his feet, but it still knocked the wind out of him. He released his grapples and slid down the wall, landing clumsily on a mantelpiece.

Thomas scanned the ceiling, desperately trying to find his prey. Footsteps approached from above, and Cain charged down the wall with a sinister grin. With a shout, Thomas leaped from the mantel just in time to dodge a ramming blow from above. He rolled over his shoulder on the rough, gravelly floor and came up running between a crevice formed by two boulders. He spun to face his foe as Cain leaped from the mantel to the floor.

Cain leaped into the crevice, and Thomas braced to parry a high blow. But he leaped to the side, onto the wall of the crevice, and launched forward while running sideways, attacking Thomas in a bizarre, angular manner.

Thomas slashed desperately at Cain's feet, but he flipped from the boulder, landed on the opposite side, and attacked Thomas in a mirrored fashion. In his desperate parrying retreat, Thomas shuffled out of the crevice and tripped over a loose stone, tumbling onto his back. Cain prepared to leap onto him, but Thomas launched his grapple and dragged himself across the ground to safety.

Thomas scrambled onto his feet but did not retract his grapple. He launched his other grapple in a different direction and ducked and weaved through the rocky terrain. His tethers crisscrossed over one another on his roundabout path as Cain pursued and attacked relentlessly from odd angles. Thomas ducked around a corner and was met with a savage kick as Cain had headed him off. He was knocked back onto his arse against the large meteor that had pierced the ceiling over a century ago.

Cain said, panting, “I’ve gotta say, little Marrow, you put up more of a fight than your old man, regardless of how futile your fight is. It’s a shame you trained so hard and for so long just to fail now.” He stepped forward, brandishing his blade to strike.

“When you fought my father,” Thomas said, “you didn’t even close in until you had worn him out. You only entered the fray when you knew he was too exhausted to blink. I still have just enough energy to flex my symbioid one last time.”

Cain hesitated as a sinewy tether wrapped around his feet. In panic, his gaze darted around the area. Layers of crisscrossed tethers zipped shut, tightening around him before he could react, trapping him, suspended from the ground, like a fly in a web.

Thomas laughed and shifted himself upwards, wiping blood from his nose.

“Release me, you whelp!” Cain bellowed.

Thomas smacked him across the face.

"I make the demands here, you son of a bitch! Where is my sister?"

"Do you have any idea what kind of hell you're about to unleash on yourself?"

Thomas smacked him again.

"My sister!"

Cain shied back. "We sold her."

"To who?" Thomas's knuckles went white gripping his sword.

"The Night Mother's crime ring. She uses little children for interference … Most don't survive more than a few years. Your sister, she must be dead by now."

Thomas reached up and grabbed Cain's throat. "Where can I find the Night Mother?"

"I don't know!" He coughed through the chokehold. "My boss, the one who took your father's symbioid, only he knows how to contact her, but I swear, your sister is dead. No child survives the Night Mother's tasks!"

Thomas's grip on Cain's throat tightened. "Then vengeance is all I require. Who is your boss? Where can I find him?"

"He's in Masonville; he runs the Symbicate. You have no idea what you're getting yourself into, boy!"

"HIS NAME!"

"His …" He coughed. "His name is …"

There was a gunshot—Cain's head snapped back, suspended dead in Thomas's grapples as crimson painted the boulders behind him.

Thomas spun around to look for the threat. He relaxed his hold on Cain and unspooled his grapples, ready to move and fight. But he dropped his guard when he saw a man in a maroon frock coat perched on a boulder by one of the blown-out glass windows.

The newcomer stood, saluting Thomas, a modified blunderbuss smoking in his arms, its trumpeted muzzle fitted with a funnel device that narrowed the barrel at the end.

"Snipes, you jammed gear! He was about to tell me what I needed to know!" Thomas bellowed.

"Cool your boiler, Hooks!" Snipes yelled, jumping down.

He made his way through the boulders, which were being filtered through by a team of other Hired Heroes as they reached the enraged Thomas.

"Boss is gonna wanna have words with you—you threw the duchess off a cliff!" Snipes started disassembling his gun.

"She had an aero-break!" Thomas protested.

"She fell into the water, Hooks. Our client will not be pleased."

"Screw the client. This man was going to tell me who was responsible for having my father killed!"

The other Hired Heroes exchanged glances. Snipes removed his shooting goggles, letting his short red hair free from his cap, and eyed Thomas coolly. "That still wasn't the job, Hooks."

"You're too narrow-minded, Snipes. You'd complete the mission at the expense of all else, even after last time!"

Snipes scowled. "Even so, I reckon Boss is still gonna wanna have words with you. Come on, Hooks, don't make me force you."

Thomas sighed in irritation. "Fine! And when we talk, I'm going to request a little holiday."

"Where to, Hooks?" another of the Hired Heroes asked.

"Masonville."

CHAPTER 2

Tara Night

Tara crept through the ancient, dusty vent like a lithe wraith in the darkness.

How can vents provide fresh air when they're so dusty? she mused as the caked dust on her damp brow mud-ified and ran into her eye.

She blinked away the stinging pain and pushed on. Of course, she didn't feel like a wraith in the darkness. She felt clumsy and sweaty and gross. She always had. That would change tonight.

She had spent all of her life as a child thief under the Night Mother and survived to come of age and progress to the next phase of employment—assassination. After rigorous training, Tara had been handed her first assignment. The child thief outside had informed her that her target—Mart Logran, union boss for the Miner's Guild—was out for the night. All she had to do was slither in through the stone vents above his loft and poison his favourite whisky.

Can I actually do this? Her mind ran with constant doubts.

She thought of her informant outside.

I can't stay on and keep an eye on those tiny tots if I don't do this. Can't help anyone if the Night Mother kills me for failing her ... Perhaps assassinating this Logran fella is a small price to pay ... I'm sure he is evil. Would have to be, to be associated with the Night Mother and piss her off.

She popped open the wooden vent cover and scraped herself the last of the way into the dark office below. She slipped through, keeping a grip on the lip of the vent as she lowered herself down, gracefully.

Then lost her grip and slammed onto the desk.

STUPID GIRL! The Night Mother's piercing cry during training rang throughout her mind and stung her more than the fall.

After a tense moment of holding her breath, she relaxed.

No commotions, no shouts or alarms, just a quiet, dark loft. No one was home—her informant was correct.

She groaned as she struggled up, rubbing her ribs through the black leather garment she wore to slip through the vents. They were torn and sanded back by the granules of the stone, but other than a few scuffs, she was fine. She tucked a stray brown hair behind her hood and hopped off the desk.

Silent, like a ninja!

She slithered into the shadows clinging to the sides of the room, searching for the bar.

There!

She slithered back to the far side of the desk, unnecessarily—no one was here. But she needed to have fun, to flex her skills, to distract herself from her task.

She reached the bar and uncorked the half-empty whisky bottle.

Perhaps I should think of it as half full? But that was hard. The only reason she survived all of these years was the drive to look out for her fellow child thieves … and even then, many did not make it. She decided it was indeed half empty.

She removed the vial from her sash, flipped the lid, and went to tip it into the whisky.

Can I actually do this?

She took in the darkened room, the rim of the poison vial quivering against that of the whisky bottle as she took in a snapshot of the life of the man she was about to assassinate … about to murder.

Trinkets and cased trophies adorned the walls.

Perhaps they were gifts from grateful people, or friends or dear family. Or perhaps they were trophies taken from those he hunted.

Framed photos in the dark of numerous smiling people, arms around one another.

Friends, loved ones … or his inner circle of criminals?

Then she took in the darkened desk she had so clumsily fallen onto, cluttered with letters and ledgers and books of all kinds, piled high on each side.

Letters of affection from loved ones? Contracts outlining his outstanding work in the community … or perhaps books on debts from the unfortunates of this town? I can't do this …

Then she thought of that poor little street child working as her point of contact outside. In the frigid mountain air, with calloused feet on rough-cut stone pavers, hungry, dirty, and alone.

If I don't do this, I'll have to abandon that child ...

She took in a deep breath, steeling herself, and tipped the vial's contents into the whisky. The clear liquid acquiesced into the lovely oaken liquor.

"There," she breathed, her voice delicate and sweet despite her task, "I'm an Assassin of the Night now."

She corked the whisky and placed it back in the bar, securing the now-empty vial in her sash, and moved to the desk to exit through the open vent. She had one foot on the desk when she froze.

Footsteps ...

Big footsteps ...

Heading towards the office door ...

She hurriedly leaped for the lip of the vent, but in her haste, in the darkness, she jumped right into the wooden grate hanging perpendicular from the ceiling. It clobbered her in the face, and she fell heavily onto the desk—again.

STUPID GIRL!

She scrambled frantically, scattering the desk clutter about the floor as she tried to right herself.

"Who's there?" A deep, powerful voice boomed from the opening office door.

A man entered, turning the dial on the gas lamps, illuminating the room with a warm glow. Illuminating Tara, hanging above the desk by her fingertips from the swinging grate.

"Stop!" the man bellowed as he launched towards her.

He was huge, tall with a barrel chest, pale, bald, and wearing a beige suit. He moved like a lumbering mass. Tara was sure she would have enough time to climb into the vent before he reached her.

She, of course, was wrong.

With half of her body pulled into the vent, the target dove over the desk. He tackled Tara in the gut and dragged her from sweet escape with a sudden yelp as she was yanked free and driven into the ground. They hit the floor with a crash. Tara had the wind knocked from her as the man's shoulder drove into her gut with all of his weight behind him.

He's a cogrusted mountain!

He rolled off her dazed and struggled to his knees, having knocked his head in the tackle.

Remember your training, no time to feel pain, no time to think. Quick strikes, evade the slow hammer blow.

Steeling herself for the second time that night, she tucked away the fact that she could not breathe, that her insides felt crushed and bruised, and she struck up from the ground, kicking him swiftly in the nose. He fell to the side with a grunt, and Tara took the opportunity to hop up onto her feet. She forced her chest to heave, regardless of her winded state. It was agony.

Just breathe. The key is to just breathe.

Her lungs burning, she jabbed the giant as he indomitably rose onto his knees a second time. Her wrist sprained when her fist bounced off his shiny head. She groaned, he growled, and he balled his ham fist and punched towards her gut. She just had the time to sidestep the blow and quickly jabbed him again with her good hand, spinning around with her continued momentum to hook-kick him across the cheek. The blows caused him to wince but were ultimately ineffective. Before allowing herself to become entangled, she bolted for the door, vaulting the table.

The desk crashed behind her, and her leg was hit by something. She faceplanted solidly and turned, straining through the white vision of pain to see that the lumbering giant had flipped the heavy wooden table, clipping her foot before she could make for the door. He clambered awkwardly over the upturned desk, nursing his grazed and bruised face.

"I'm going to make you pay for that, you blighter!" he screamed.

Tara desperately scrambled through the spread-out clutter, searching for something, anything to defend herself. He reached down and grabbed her leg—she reached out and grabbed a desk lamp. He pulled her towards him and bent down to punch her in the head with his giant ham fist. She brought the lamp around, swinging wildly with a scream, and shattered the glass bulb of the lamp across his face. He howled in pain but did not release her, so she kicked him in the groin with her free leg, and his grip loosened enough for her to struggle free and make for the door again.

She turned and rose onto all fours and bolted into a sprint. But he reached out and grabbed her by the back of her hood. He pulled violently, yanking her hair, and threw her back over the overturned table. She landed in a heap, winded yet again.

Oh cogrust, you stupid, clumsy girl.

The man lumbered around the desk, but this time there was nothing she could do—she was thoroughly beaten.

"Now I'm going to teach you some manners, you little bastar ..." He stopped as he loomed over her for the finishing blow.

She looked up, flicking the dark hair from her eyes. Her hood had come free when he tossed her over the table.

"Why … why, you're just a young girl!"

Tara spat blood and tried to scramble away.

"Hold on, hold on, hold on!" he fussed.

He stepped forward and grabbed at her again, but his whole demeanour had changed. His snarl turned from one of rage to that of a smiling man … albeit one with blood running down his face.

"I thought you were some thug or hoodlum coming in here to cause me grief. Why, I bet you were just looking for a reprieve from the cold, eh?" he said gently, crouching down.

Tara said nothing, staring up at the man in disbelief, cradling her sprained wrist and bruised side.

"Please forgive me!" he said, taking her sprained wrist. She recoiled. "Don't worry, I can fix that up proper. Come on, up you get. I'll take good care of you."

He helped her up and pulled up his plush desk chair for her to sit in. Then he grabbed one of the hard-backed wooden chairs from the side and placed it by the comfy chair to sit on as he inspected her hand.

"Gee, you sure did bang that wrist up nice, huh? I do have a thick skull, or so my secretary says." He chuckled.

Tara tentatively chuckled with him. *He seems lovely.*

"Now, what's your story, luv?" He pulled a handkerchief from his coat pocket and wrapped it around her wrist. "Don't worry, I don't use it. Just a gift from the matron of an orphanage I helped out once. Felt bad not to carry it around with me. She spent so long sewing 'thank you' into it."

She looked down at the red cloth with white letters etched into the corner.

"Not much for talking, eh? I can't blame you after I spear tackled you into the ground." He chuckled. "How about a drink? Would that take the edge off?"

Tara nodded tentatively. He smiled and rose, heading towards the bar with lumbering steps. He wiped his face on the sleeve of his beige suit and raised his eyebrows in surprised admiration.

"You've got some fight to you, young miss, not surprising. I bet you grew up on the streets, poor thing. I tell you what." He poured oaken-coloured liquor into two tumblers. "If you tell me your name, I'll buy you a hot meal."

"Tara," she mumbled.

"Tara!" he said, turning towards her and lumbering over. "What a lovely name. My name is Mart, Mart Logran. My friends call me 'The Log,' for obvious reasons." He smiled again, big and beaming. "You look like you've experienced more than your years would say. How old are you?"

"I think I'm eighteen," Tara said, not knowing entirely for sure.

"Eighteen, and hard enough to fight a man three times your size!" He handed her the tumbler and sat down. The chair groaned in protest under his weight, but it held firm for its master, for its charming master.

You know, I think I won't go through with this assassination after all, she thought. Her mind turned to the wrath of the Night Mother, but she felt as if this man could provide some protection.

"We'll have this drink, get cleaned up, then I'll take you to this great little eatery I know of. They do warm, hearty soups, and their coffee is just to die for, and I want to hear all about you, Tara. But for now, to new friends!" He raised the glass.

"To new friends!" Tara said, relaxing.

In habit, she raised the glass to her lips.

POISON!

"Wait!" she called out ... but it was too late.

Mart 'The Log' Logran slumped to the floor like a ragdoll. Dead.

"Fuck!" She dropped the glass and palmed her face. "Tara, you moon rock moron, lump of wet coal, girl!"

She rose from her chair, fighting the urge to vomit, and made for the vent. She remembered her first kill, an older child thief who tried to rob her and her friend. He got violent, she pushed back, and he slipped and hit his head on the gutter. A stupid accident that had put her on the Night Mother's watch. Now she had done it again.

At least I won't have to face the wrath of the Night Mother. I can still help my child thieves.

She slinked out from the disordered room.

#

It was a crisp night. Cold mountain air breezed through the streets of Copper Copple as Tara slinked outside. The buildings were packed tightly into the carved flat that the city was built on, here on the mountain's peak. They had sheer, slanted roofs to displace the snow, and the gas streetlamps with copper fittings lit the cobblestone with cosy warmth in defiance of the chill.

Tara shivered as she made her way down the street, passing a sleeping paper boy who had stuffed his coat with the unsold copies of the day. Some were still laid out on display—paper weighted with bits and pieces. The headlines leaped out at her in bold black letters.

"Mart 'The Log' Logran plants his roots against poor mining conditions!"

"Well," she lamented with a hiss of misted breath, "it was too much to hope he was a scoundrel."

She scuttled down an alleyway to meet her informant. The cool air was sending shivers across her body as it chilled her sweat, and she sighed with relief when the kid emerged with her clothes.

The kid handed her a bundle, her brown leather military coat, and she hurriedly put it on. It draped her entire body down to her ankles. She tied it tight with the cord around her waist and donned the baggy leather hood she had sewn into it. She finished the look with a long red scarf wrapped around her neck.

"Any word, little urchin?" she asked, handing him a sweet from her coat pocket.

"I tried to send a signal when he turned up, miss. I'm sorry, but a dog scared me off."

"That's okay, little one. I handled him." She suppressed a shudder. "Any word, though?"

"Yes," he gazed around uneasily, "one of the other assassins found me, said she wanted to speak with you, right now."

A sense of dread crept down her spine, something far colder than the chilled sweat.

"Thanks, little one. Take this and go buy some food for you and your brother." She handed him a pale blue cube.

He took it greedily and scrambled away.

Tara sighed. She should have known she was being observed from an adjacent rooftop somewhere. Billie would have watched the whole thing through the windows, would have watched her hesitate to poison the whisky, and would have watched her flail about fighting poor Mart …

She hardened her resolve, and made her way to the rooftops, climbing up gutters and escape stairs and lower buildings.

She climbed the lip of the rooftop; the woodsmoke left its impression on the clear mountain air and cast a sinister veil over the pale green luminescence of the shattered moon. The Night was waiting for her on the first rooftop she picked. Billie had probably moved to meet her there; still, it was unnerving.

"Had yourself quite the tussle there, little sister." The young woman emerged from the shadows. Her hood was black silk and covered most of her face; beneath, she wore bulky, blue-tinted goggles embedded in a leather mask wrapped around all but her nose and jaw, revealing olive skin, pale from a life of the night. Tara was more unnerved by those blue-tinted orbs than whatever weapons she knew the woman possessed. "Report?" One of the goggles whirred with tiny moving gears, the symbioid woven into them zooming a lens to pick out micro expressions as Tara answered.

"Billie." Tara nodded with respect to her trainer. "The deed is done. Mart Logran is dead. My street contact couldn't get the signal to me that he was on his way up. There was no choice but to fight him," she said, belying her dread.

"That was due to my design."

Tara tried to suppress the urge to grind her teeth. "You sent the dog that scared my contact off?"

"You knew we would test you, sweet Tara. I was instructed not only to see if you had it in you to kill on purpose, but to do it with the target right in front of you. The Night Mother expected him to kill you, or for you to claw your way to survival. What I witnessed, however ..."

Tara filled the silence with her fretting fears, waiting for the reprimand, for dozens of assassins to emerge from the shadows and strike her down.

"Mother would say it was truly ingenious, managing to win his trust and then getting him to drink the poison right in front of you. 'What a way to confirm a hit!' she would say, but we know I know better."

Tara bit her lip. "Oh?"

"You're still too soft, Tara."

"Maybe I'm just a bad assassin."

Billie giggled, a strangely innocent sound. "Please, Tara, you know the truth even if you can't accept it. Your skills could rival even mine if not for your heart getting in the way. If you want to survive, you need to do what I did, kill that side of you. The Night Mother will accept nothing less."

"Maybe I could bury it," Tara shivered, "but I don't think I could ever kill it like you did."

Billie hesitated. "Perhaps that is enough for now. Come, little sister, let us away to the Den. I must report what I witnessed to Mother; then she will decide our fate."

"Our?"

"I did train you after all ... our fates are linked. Come." Billie turned from Tara and all but vanished into the smoky shadows as she traversed the rooftops and gaps between the clustered buildings.

Tara sighed and reluctantly followed.

CHAPTER 3

Eric Futruble

Eric eyed his competition with the air of practiced smug nobility, comparing his hand to the other potential hands around the table. A cluster of warm-coloured cubes lay in a disorganised heap on the blue felt surface between them—yellows, bright oranges, and even a few darkening amber colours.

High stakes indeed, Eric thought.

"Are you going to throw in anytime soon, young prince?" the gruff man asked from the side of the table. His giant, flabby arms bulged over the rim and spilled over the felt.

"Hmm? Prince?" Eric looked around in a show of confusion. Then he turned his attention back with a smile. "Oh, how kind of you, dear fellow. I might look princely, but I am just a lowly viscount's son. This cloak, however ..."

He gestured to his pale green tailcoat with gold lace trimmings and polished silver buttons, "this actually was a gift from the prince. A bribe really to let him beat me in a tennis match while his new fiancée was watching." He laughed deeply. "Of course, she had her eyes on me the whole time, didn't watch us play for the sport, if you catch my drift."

The players around the table sniggered, but not the fat one.

"You're stalling, Viscount! Either make your bet or fold like the flop you are!"

More sniggers.

Eric made a show of looking hurt and glanced at his cards. Two towers and a keep. He scanned the cards arrayed on the table: a gatehouse, a wall, and a moon spire.

Enough to make a full castle.

Eric twirled the single gold lock of hair falling over his brow. Two of the gamblers exchanged shifty looks. Then he picked up two amber cubes—the last of his money—and tossed them into the pot. They clattered into the haphazard mess of cubes, causing some to shift and slide into each other, turning into deeper, warmer shades.

This is getting expensive.

"All in!" he said, beaming his smug smile.

As they went around the table, the others threw their lots into the game. Fat Arms folded like most of the others. Only two others went all in, the two with shifty eyes who Eric had his sights on.

"All right, gentlemen ..." the dealer said.

"If you could call us that, really." Eric beamed smugly again.

Fat Arms rolled his eyes.

"Show us your hands," the dealer continued, unperturbed.

Shifty Eyes One laid down his hand with a sinister grin, peering up from underneath his bandana mischievously. Two lookout towers and a town watch.

Shifty Eyes Two cursed and threw down his cards, but Eric did not miss the knowing look they shared.

"We have an established settlement," the dealer said. "Only a fort or a castle can contend."

"Well," Eric said in mock shock, "that is a nice little town you've got there, Mister Person. It would look nice next to my castle!" Eric threw down his cards, and the gamblers gasped.

"We have a full castle. The game goes to the prince's wife's lover," the dealer said.

"You've got a cheek," Eric said playfully, reaching in and tossing him an orange cube.

"Sir." The dealer pocketed it and gathered the cards while Shifty Eyes One and Two leaped up enraged.

"That can't be! We figured out your tell—you twirled your stupid little hair whenever you had a bad hand!"

Eric put on his mock shock. "A bad hand? I tell you, Mister Person. I have never had a bad hand. Every hand I had has led me to this victory. A bad hand is simply a stepping-stone."

"I'll cut that pretty lock off, along with your scalp, you cheat!" Shifty Eyes Two said, drawing a long, curved knife.

"Gentlemen, please!" the dealer said, as two burly bouncers waltzed up behind him from the dim, pipe-smoke-filled gambling den. "There will be no cutting of locks or scalps at my table. Please take your grievances outside."

"Sure thing, Mister Dealer," Eric said, scooping the cubes together, sliding them into each other to form even darker and darker shades of amber, until finally, they turned a slight shade of red. "Gee, this is a fortune, eh? I'm sure you two would like a chance to have it back?" he said to the two gamblers as the bouncers escorted them outside.

"Another game?" the one with the bandana asked as he wrapped his dingy coat around his waist, with sweat seeping through his vest.

"Not against the long con that you can play," the one with the knife said. He didn't have a coat, which struck Eric as odd in this town, but the armed man had a woolly jumper, which he tied around his neck.

"First of all," Eric said harshly as they stepped out onto the chilly street, the cold cobblestone echoing their footsteps throughout the tall, shanty buildings lining the alley, "I won fair and square. And second of all, I can't stand people who tie their jumpers around their necks like that; either wear it or don't. Make up your mind. Be a man! Third of all, I want to trade these winnings for information."

The two exchanged looks.

While he hesitantly untied his jumper and bundled it under his arm, the armed man asked, "What kind of information?"

"The smuggling kind. I heard of an exotic animal being smuggled into this town last night. I want to buy it."

"That animal has already been sold," the one with the bandana said.

Knife Man scolded him.

"Ah, so you two do know of it! Excellent. I know it's been sold, and for its intended purpose, but I also know it hasn't been transported to those ruffians yet. I'll give you half of these cubes now, half once the beast has been transported to my estate safely."

"Or," the one with the knife brandished it menacingly, "we kill you, take the cubes, and sell the beast to our buyer anyway."

Eric sighed. "If you must."

The thug lunged forward to drive the knife straight into Eric's heart. Eric took a deep breath and flexed the *living* symbioid woven throughout his entire body. He evaporated into thousands of tiny little tendrils and *saw* their journey as if each had its own vision and swam through the atmosphere to connect again behind the lunging man. They wove together, forming Eric with his blade drawn, facing the back of his attacker.

Dissolving and writhing through the air in a million wriggling pieces—that's what it felt like—and it was a straining process. But from anyone else's point of view, he was simply gone and back again. He had blinked out of and then back into existence.

"What?" the one with the bandana gasped.

But he could do nothing as Eric swiftly stabbed the exposed attacker in the back.

He fell with a wet cry and tumbled onto the cold ground. Eric withdrew his weapon and quickly spun on the bandana-wearing man, putting the dripping crimson blade to his neck and forcing him up against the wall of the dark alley.

"A living symbioid?"

"Pfft," Eric said with a huff. "So archaic. I think we prefer the terms *mechanical* and *conscious* to dead and living symbioids, don't you?"

"It's not right, letting something like that into your body!"

Eric laughed coldly, all mock bravado fading. "You let me worry about what is right, Mister Bandana." All mirth seeped from his voice, and sweat dripped down his brow, as if every fibre of his being had just sprinted independently of each other. "Now hush. I don't like having to do that kind of thing, and you idiots made me do it, so cooperate, or I'll take my anger out on you."

"You don't like blinking?"

"Stabbing people," Eric said, shaking off a minor bout of dizziness. Eric's uncle had told him the dizziness would subside with more use. That was when it was gifted to him years ago. Uncle was wrong. It troubled Eric, but the blink was invaluable. "Now show me where this beastie is, or I'll cut your throat."

#

Twenty minutes later, Eric, led by the even sweatier Mister Bandana and followed by two dozen constables with blunderbusses, were en route to a warehouse on the border of Shanty Towers and the Banking District, where the middle and upper classes of Quartrant clashed.

Eric always marvelled at the quaint clusters of three-storey-high shanty buildings, and how they were suddenly stopped short by the sheer, imposing wall of the much larger skyline of white. Here the black and brown of Shanty Towers broke upon the cool white clay of the Banking District. He marvelled over how two worlds could collide yet coexist, could be a part of each other and yet be … apart.

Gas lamps lining the streets lit the cool night air, pushing through the light fog that rolled in without the strength to impede visibility. The shattered moon spilled across the night with a veiled pale green lustre.

Mister Bandana led them to a cellar door beside the warehouse and went to open it. The sergeant in his dark police cape halted him.

"Are we to expect any surprises down there?" His bushy moustache trembled with every syllable.

"Nay, sir, we thought that guards would draw attention."

"You left the Baulsaw alone?" Eric gasped.

Mister Bandana lowered his gaze. "Yes, sir."

"Idiot, what if it got loose? It would tear this town apart!" Eric shoved him out of the way and threw open the cellar doors. There was a dark stone staircase leading into the depths beneath the warehouse.

"All right, lads," the bushy moustache-bearing sergeant said. "Let's get a move on."

He tightened the strap of his custodian helm and ushered his constables down into the cellar, and one took Mister Bandana down with them. Before he entered, Eric grabbed the last constable.

"Johnson, is it?"

"Aye, sir!" the young, wide-eyed officer said. "How did you remember my name, sir? If you don't mind me asking?"

Eric glanced up from the officer's name badge with a smile. "I always remember the names of useful men."

Johnson beamed.

The sergeant rolled his eyes.

"Now, Johnson," Eric said, gripping his shoulder tight, "I have a gut feeling. Do you know where my estate is, the one at the end of Billows Lane?"

The constable nodded. "Aye, sir ..." He blushed. "I follow the tabloids."

Eric grinned. "Nothing wrong with that. Now, I want you to run to my estate, inform my butler of what is going on, and have him set up my boat on the docks to receive a Baulsaw in a hurry. Step to, Constable!"

"Aye, sir!" Johnson saluted and jostled away from the cellar doors into the night.

"You have a way with people, Mister Futruble. I wonder if you'd teach me a thing or two when we have a spare moment?" The sergeant leaned against the brick wall, crossing his arms.

Eric straightened, readjusting the yellow scarf around his neck along with his pale green coat. "People are easy, Sergeant Matchins; you just need to make them feel as if they are contributing," Eric said, smiling. "Now, would you please lead the way. I'd feel more comfortable having a trained officer lead me into the depths."

Matchins rolled his eyes again. "As you say, Mister Futruble."

Eric stood back and gestured to the cellar with a flourish, admiring Matchins's moustache and broad shoulders.

Not bad, he thought.

The stairs led to a cellar with a high ceiling beneath the warehouse. The constables had lit the lamps around the supporting pillars on the sides. In the centre of the large, empty space was a tarp covering something as large as two wagons. There was a furnace burning on the far side, keeping the room warm with an eerie red glow.

There was a breath coming from beneath the tarp, the snoring of a large animal.

"Get that furnace put out," Eric ordered one of the constables, who quickly scuttled to obey him.

"Why the furnace, sir?" Matchins asked.

"Baulsaws are reptilian, much like the other species that dwell with it on those tropical islands. They need heat to get going, but the Baulsaw is unique in the sense that once it gets going, its own mass and movement generate enough heat for it to stay active indefinitely. I'd rather keep it cold."

"Sound reasoning, sir. All right, lads, let's get that tarp off, confirm it's the real article."

Two officers removed the tarp. It slid gracefully into a clump on the floor to reveal a sleeping hulk within a cage of iron. The creature was huge, built like a bull, the animals from farms half a country away. It had powerful, bulky legs and a short, thick tail. It was covered in green and red scales and had a bowed head hanging from titanic shoulders and two enormous antlers that scraped the cage bars with every heave of its snoring.

"Whistling steam," one of the constables gaped, "that's a big cogrusted animal!"

Eric's gut turned.

Something was wrong.

"Mister Bandana," he said in a low voice.

"My name is Edward."

"Where are the reinforcements on that cage?"

Across the room, the constable Eric had sent opened the furnace hatch with a loud creak. The Baulsaw shifted.

"Reinforcements, Viscount? I don't know what you mean. That there is a wrought-iron cage."

The constable doused the fire with a pail of water, killing the heat with a steaming splutter. Other constables started dragging large chains noisily across the cavernous space to hitch onto the cage so it could be hauled above through the warehouse trapdoor.

And it was still far too warm in here.

"You fool! A Baulsaw that size will tear that cage apart! Everybody freeze!"

The officers dragging the chains halted. The constable lowering the hatch on the furnace froze.

"If that beast awakes before it cools down, it will break free and destroy half of the city, probably. We need to all slowly drop what we are doing, get that tarp over the cage, and then wait for it to cool down in here."

The officers slowly set down the chains and hatches of the furnace, and several slowly made their way to the tarp to drape it over the large cage. A much harder feat to do quietly, compared to removing it.

"Oh, bullocks," Matchins said.

"What is it, Sergeant?" Eric spun.

"I sent a man upstairs to open the trapdoor ..."

All eyes slowly turned towards the ceiling.

The trapdoor dropped open with a large click and fell. It swung wildly on its hinges and knocked into two of the pillars with a mighty clang that echoed throughout the room.

The Baulsaw shifted.

All eyes turned towards it. No one made a sound.

"All good down there?" the officer up above called.

This was the straw that broke the Baulsaw's back.

The Baulsaw's eyes shot open, yellow and brilliant and terrifying. It reared up, shaking the cage and rattling it almost to pieces.

"Get that tarp on!" Eric shouted.

"Fire on the beast!" one of the constables bellowed.

"No!"

Eric tried to stop them, but their blunderbusses started to go off with their ridiculous trumpeting sounds, shooting into the poor caged creature, serving only to enrage it as the shots merely scratched the surface of its tough scales and hide.

The beast lurched forward, smashing the iron bars to bits.

The constable who had doused the furnace was the first to be gored by its antlers. Then Mister Bandana fell under its trampling foot. It barrelled straight for Matchins and Eric. Straight for the only exit it could see.

Matchins kept his cool, took a knee, and fired straight into the beast's head. It clipped an antler, causing a pitiful amount to crumble away. Eric grabbed Matchins just as the Baulsaw was upon them and blinked them both to the side. The dizzy weariness set in as he disassembled into tendrils and swam through the air with not just his own body, but Matchins's as well. They fell in a heap to one side a split second later. The constable tried to throw up. Eric rolled to one side, panting with a sheen of fresh sweat as the Baulsaw forced its way up the narrow staircase and burst through onto the city street.

Several brave constables charged after it while reloading their clumsy weapons, and several stayed behind to deal with the wounded and the dead.

"What the hell just happened? I can't breathe, everything hurts!" Matchins was rambling. A common side effect when people are suddenly blinked for the first time.

Eric sighed, leaned over him and slapped him hard across the face. "Sergeant, your men need you to focus!"

Matchins shot up, shaking off his shock. "Apologies, sir, that was unbecoming."

What a man!

"I need you to get your men to drive the beast towards me. If Johnson got to my butler in time, we can trap it on my boat, then ship it home. Hop to, Sergeant!"

Eric went to sprint up the stairway, which was clogged with men reloading their blunderbusses and taking aim through the cellar doors onto the beast on the streets.

"I sure wish I could blink through walls."

Eric looked to the open loading bay trapdoor up above and blinked up there instead. But not before he retrieved the bandana from Mister Bandana's corpse. Upon blinking up into the warehouse, he found a wide-eyed officer, who frantically asked, "What happened?"

"The beast got out. Go support your fellow officers, constable." Eric blinked away before he could reply.

With every step out of blinking into reality, he could feel his muscles, his tendons, his very bones aching. His lungs burned.

But he had to push on.

He blinked out an open window and onto a rooftop over the street. The beast was breaking through walls and houses, tossing lampposts and signs about like they were nothing.

One unlucky wagon driver veered out of the way of a thrown lamppost just in time. It struck the side wheel, and he hightailed it down a side street with a listing carriage over the cobblestones. Several officers burst out of the cellar door onto the streets in pursuit of the Baulsaw and fired again, which drew its attention back towards them.

Before it could charge, Eric whistled. The beast followed the source of the noise. Its wide eyes narrowed as it homed in on Eric, who was brandishing the red bandana from the smuggler.

The Baulsaw's nostrils flared.

"Good, he remembers the scent of this idiot."

The Baulsaw leaped up the wall, breaking into the second storey of a shanty tower and rocking the building to its meagre foundations. A second later, it burst through the ceiling onto the roof by Eric, and turned this way and that, searching for the scent.

"Well, blimey, I did not expect that!"

The beast reared on him and charged.

Eric blinked away.

He blinked from rooftop to street side to dark alleyway, drawing the Baulsaw into the Banking District, away from where people would be sleeping and revelling at this hour of the night.

"Now, if I lead this creature through the Banking District, I might accidentally damage my accountant's office," Eric said between heaving breaths in an effort to keep calm while drawing the hulking monster towards him. "That would certainly annoy him ... Excellent." He smirked.

He blinked up onto the side of the next building, his growing dizziness nearly causing him to stumble. But he caught himself.

He spun around, searching for the docks.

They were close, maybe one or two blinks away.

"Nearly there, don't give in to the burning just yet, boy."

The Baulsaw crashed into the building below him, causing it to shake and Eric to fall.

The ground rushed up to meet him. Just before impact, he had the wherewithal to blink away. Eric slammed into the side of a building in the adjacent alleyway, knocking the wind from him before stumbling onwards.

The Baulsaw followed, relentless.

Eric burst through the other end of the alleyway onto the docks. There were crowds of officers and reporters who had parted away towards Eric's family ship on the first wharf. Out in front of the wharf, a wooden container had been set out, its dark opening beckoning Eric inwards.

"Get the hell back, you imbeciles!" Eric shouted as he blinked into the container.

The people screamed as the Baulsaw crashed through the narrow exit to the alley and stomped around looking for its prey. It sighted him—down the human corridor—Eric was waving the red bandana from within the container.

It charged. This time Eric did not blink away. The wharf rattled as the Baulsaw bounded closer with each giant step, trembling as if the world was shaking. It entered the mouth of the container. And just before impact, Eric blinked outward through the entrance, past the rampaging creature.

It impacted the other side with a titanic crash, and the wooden sides of the container fell away to reveal a reinforced iron cage. Men rushed in from the sides and closed the front of the cage, sealing the Baulsaw in place.

"Let him stew in this place for a while until he cools down enough to slumber. Then load the poor creature on board and send him home." Eric rasped the semi-coherent command to one of the dockworkers, his face red and wet from his exertions. The Baulsaw reared against the bars, trying to break free again, but this cage was too strong. Soon it would give up and rest.

"And for pity's sake, put a tarp over the thing!" Matchins ordered as he rushed through the crowd with his constables catching up behind him. He seemed to be uninjured.

The dockworkers moved to obey, and Eric turned to the sergeant with a smile.

"How did you fare, Officer?" Eric cocked his head.

Their conversation was cut short as the reporters rushed in, snapping photographs on their box cameras, flashing them with their enormous fluorescent devices, and the cacophony of shutters closing was replaced by gears whirring as the cameras reset themselves.

"Viscount, how does it feel to save Quartrant?" an eager reporter asked from the throng.

"Will you accept another key to the city from the mayor?"

"What are your romantic plans, Viscount Futruble? How can you still be such an eligible bachelor while being a hero of the city three times over?"

Eric raised his hands. "Please! Please, I would not be able to do the work I do if it were not for the fine efforts of our police force, with men like Constable Johnson here." He gestured to the star-struck officer in the crowd.

Matchins suppressed a laugh, returning to his serious visage within an instant.

The reporters turned to Johnson, who gasped, open-mouthed and wide-eyed.

"He'll be happy to answer any of your questions while I escort this beast back to the Baul Islands!" While the reporters were distracted, Eric grabbed the sergeant and blinked onto the boat as the Baulsaw was hauled onto it and the steam started billowing from the exhaust stack.

"Cogrust." Matchins swayed, and Eric helped him grip the railing.

"Terribly sorry, Sergeant. I was hoping to have a word with you in private."

Down on the dock the reporters were pestering the young constable with questions; none of them had noticed Eric absconding with the sergeant.

"That poor lad is going to say something stupid, and I'll never hear the end of it." Matchins sighed.

"We all make sacrifices to obtain good things." Eric reached out and smoothed Matchins's moustache, and Matchins glanced Eric up and down.

"And what good things are you talking about, Viscount?"

"You can call me Eric, Sergeant."

Matchins's serious visage broke for another second, letting a sly smirk creep up the corner of his mouth. "I did not take you for that sort, Eric."

"Am I wrong in taking you for that sort, Sergeant?"

The sergeant shrugged. "You can call me Walter."

Eric realised he was still playing with Walter's moustache. "Walter, let me give instructions to the captain of this vessel; then I can blink you away from the docks discreetly and you can escort me to my estate?"

"It would be my pleasure."

CHAPTER 4

Some Other Players

The Pit was arguably the lowest dreg of the slum district of Quartrant, not because it was an eatery set into a constantly damp basin, carved out of the remnants of an ineffective meteor shelter, and not because it served the rankest food and stalest liquor, but because of the sleazy way its regulars looked at you. Whether man or woman, their lecherous eyes sized you up for what they could take from you.

Eleanor was used to such looks, fighting her mother's crusade against the slavers, but these looks were *different*, even if just as foul and unnerving. She felt comfortable with her large fur coat, which covered her dark brown skin from their eyes, doubly so as she was not used to the cold here in Weznin. The coat did not hide the enormity of the sword strapped to her back, though. It poked out past her head and her dark black hair.

She stood within the basin, roofed by rotting planks and surrounded by a rickety balcony up above on the "ground" floor as the thugs and mercenaries and smugglers ate, drank, and ... leered. Her mother haggled with a bloated excuse of a man at the main table.

"So, the beast is set near the Banking District?"

"Yes, Madam Brune, yes." The smuggler belched before shoving meat into his mouth. "You really should be more trusting," he mumbled through half-chewed food.

Eleanor grimaced.

"Trusting? You think I would ever trust your kind?" Madam Brune said.

"What? You don't like indigenous Weznin?" The smuggler's skin was tanned olive in comparison with the nobility class who had migrated from the inland regions long ago, after the cataclysm. *But he is still Weznin*, Eleanor thought.

"Not Weznin, smugglers," Madam Brune scoffed.

The smuggler scoffed back, "Then don't employ us."

The entrance above burst open, and an unkempt woman hurried down. "Boss! Boss! The constables have moved in on the Baulsaw!"

The smuggler's eyes bulged out of his head. "What?"

He looked back and forth between the Brunes and the runner.

"Trust you said?" Her mother's voice rang with that tone, the tone that meant blood was about to be shed. Eleanor tensed. "I trust that you were always going to fail me." She glanced at Eleanor.

Eleanor sensed the brewing battle but kept her coat on, resisting the inevitable.

Before anyone could react, Madam Brune blurred forward, fast, faster than the eye could follow. She slashed at the messenger woman, and she was dead before she hit the ground.

As if a fuse had been struck, the den erupted into bedlam.

The thugs fired on the Brunes.

With a growl, Eleanor gripped the handle of her enormous sword and triggered the button that activated the symbioid woven into it. The sword expanded into a tower shield, shredding her nice coat and revealing her flowing powder blue dress beneath. It was strategically cut at the skirt to allow full range of motion as she crouched into position, using her sword-shield to cover herself.

A smattering of shots pinged off her defences, and the fan mechanisms collapsed, allowing her to surge forward, switching between blade and shield as needed as she cut through the hapless band of foes. Eleanor was untouchable, unstoppable, but the real threat was her mother.

Madam Brune blurred into the fray, oblivious to her daughter's separate onslaught. The battle itself was easy. They had fought many more against greater odds—it gave Eleanor time to think.

I am so tired of this life of battle under the whims of my mother. She flourished and swiped at the waist of a large bandit who leaped down from the balcony. She triggered the fan mechanism an instant before contact, and the sword-shield expanded as it cleaved him in two.

As the enemies arrayed against them dwindled, trapped in that stupid bunker establishment against foes much their superior, the lead smuggler bolted up the stairs.

"Daughter, follow him!" Eleanor heard her mother's command from across the room, and she obeyed.

#

Elsewhere, it was a cold night with a light rolling fog as Luke Sill sauntered through the Dreg-slums of Shanty Towers. The district was disreputable enough at the best of times, but even seasoned street thugs trod wearily in the Dreg-slums.

But Luke was so casual about it, he could have been walking down to the local store to get some milk.

He wore an expensive yet no-nonsense black leather military coat, which accented his tall, slender features and shaved head, with his pale scalp refracting the dim street-lights in the fog. He did not flaunt his wealth, but it was noticed by those sinister folk who happened to pass him by. As he moved confidently through the cesspools that called themselves streets, he quickly realised he had two shadows.

Continuing unperturbed, his attention was called for from the second storey of one of the shanty towers.

"Hello, handsome! Fancy spending some of that cube on a real gal?"

Luke stopped in his tracks and appreciated the fine form of the half-naked woman leaning out from the whorehouse.

"I would if I were not running late, lovely miss," he answered easily.

"You don't seem in a hurry ... are you sure you can't slip in for a while?"

Luke felt a burning desire to answer the lady's call, but a keen prickling of his senses told him to stay put.

"Things always seem to work out for me. Perhaps I'll stop by on my way back?"

She made a pouting face before poking her tongue out and withdrawing into the red-curtained room. With a smile, Luke was about to take another step when he was stopped by the unmistakable click of a blunderbuss being primed behind him.

"You seem ta walk around these here parts unaware of the shit you will walk into, rich boy," the gruff voice said.

Luke looked down to his intended next step and smirked. He was about to step into a puddle of open sewage. He turned slowly with his hands raised.

"Lucky you stopped me then, sir. Otherwise, I would have stepped into said shit."

"Oh, you've stepped into shit all right. Hand over the cubes, or I'll shoot ya gut and roll yer around the actual crap to die." The man was clothed in ragged, unwashed clothes—as was his compatriot standing a way off with his hand on a sheathed blade.

Luke's every instinct screamed to run or fight, but that prickling sense at the back of his mind urged him to stay put.

After a moment of Luke looking calmly down the wide barrel of the blunderbuss, the man with the blade spoke up, puffing steam from his breath with each slurred word. "Well, are youse just going to stands there and get shot?"

"I'm not going to get shot," Luke said.

"And what makes you so sure?" the man with the blunderbuss said, inching closer.

"Your gun is going to jam, or backfire, or even miss despite the point-blank range, and then I'll gut you and leave you in the sewage as I continue on my way," Luke answered.

"How do you figure? Ain't no one touches this gun but me, and I keep better care of it than Jimmy there does his own blade."

"How do I figure?" Luke asked. "Just a feeling I have, I suppose—call it a killer's intuition."

The one called Jimmy laughed. "Fancies himself a killer, Bobbie, perhaps we's should show's him how's us real killers behave?"

"Righto, Jimmy, righto." Bobbie raised his blunderbuss to fire. Luke did not flinch.

There was a roar and a shaking of buildings several blocks over towards the Banking District. Bobbie looked away for the briefest of seconds, and that was all the prickling told Luke he needed.

Luke lunged forward and grabbed the blunderbuss by the barrel, knocking Bobbie onto the ground with a savage right hook. He flipped the gun over in his hands and fired, hitting the former gunman in the heart.

"Shits!" Jimmy swore.

The roaring and rumbling were accompanied by gunshots and shouts in the distance. Luke marched over to Jimmy as he tried to draw his sabre, which appeared to be jammed in place.

"What's going on?" he shouted, stumbling back from the approaching Luke, who flipped over the smoking blunderbuss again, holding it like a club.

"It's my lucky day. It appears you forgot to oil your sword today, and in the chilly air, it stuck to your scabbard. How unfortunate for you though." Luke bludgeoned the faltering Jimmy to the ground and then kept bludgeoning him until he was dead.

Luke sighed and threw the bloody blunderbuss away. It clattered across the worn pavers.

"That was exciting!" a melodic voice called from on high. Luke spun to see the prostitute in the window again. "How's about a freebie for the dashing man?"

Luke groaned as he checked his pocket watch. *I'm running late as it is*, he thought.

"On my way back, miss, I promise!" She pouted and pulled her head back in through the window. "Darn it, how am I going to get there in time and take up her offer?"

As the rumbling and roaring pulled farther away from his position, it was replaced by the incessant scraping and clattering of hooves. A carriage careened around the corner from the direction he came, one wheel missing, scraping against the filthy ground. It pulled up right next to Luke.

"Good day, sir," Luke said.

"It must be my lucky day, street walker. As you can see, I have damaged my carriage, and I must make a delivery pronto to very unforgiving people—would you mind riding along with me to counterbalance away from the broken wheel?"

The prickling intensified.

"Certainly!" Luke hopped on, allowing the carriage to tilt away from the missing wheel, and the driver ushered the two horses to trot along at a decent pace.

"Where are you heading to, stranger?" the driver asked.

"Wherever you are, I assume," Luke replied. "What broke your wheel?"

"I was riding down Main Street when a gear-jamming Baulsaw broke out of nowhere! It tossed a lamppost, which shattered my wheel, and I veered down the side street and barely made it out of there alive!" the driver shouted.

Luke chuckled. "My lucky day indeed."

#

Eleanor Brune kicked the hapless smuggler out of the tavern door. It buckled under his meaty weight, and he spilled out onto the cold street. She followed his tumble, carrying her enormous sword-shield, which dripped with the crimson of the smuggling ring, and strode out into the night, holding the sword over the quivering man's gut.

Madam Brune strode out next with a pompous expression on her dark, wrinkled features and carrying a sack of purses from the dead.

Eleanor shivered in the cold. Her blue dress was form-fitting and slitted appropriately to maintain her modesty while allowing free movement. But it was ill suited to the cold, and her coat was inside, torn to shreds by her own hesitation.

"Cold, eh?" The fat smuggler laughed nervously. "There are some nice furs inside. I can barter with you?"

"We will take what we will, you cretin, after you have paid for your failure," Eleanor spat. She regretted her anger. It wasn't him she was angry at, not really.

"Sheesh, just trying to help you out. I know dark-skinned islanders hate this cold." The smuggler winced.

"But you don't seem to know that the islanders kill those who betray them," Madam Brune said. She slid the cubes from the purses together, forming deeper and darker shades as they changed from blue to green to yellow to amber, as she strode around Eleanor to look into the smuggler's eyes.

"B-betray? Me?"

"This is the second time that you let the constables halt our plans to wreak havoc on this putrid, invasive city."

"It's not my fault!" he cried.

"No, but it was your responsibility. Eleanor," Madam Brune commanded.

Eleanor drove the giant sword into the smuggler's gut—he cried out in pain. She activated the mechanical symbioid woven into the fan mechanism in the sword, and it splayed wide, becoming the giant, sharpened tower shield.

The smuggler cried again and was dead the next instant as his body was torn in two.

Eleanor retracted the fan mechanism, and the shield collapsed into a giant sword again. She shook the blood from it, and it ran off like flowing water.

"And what now, Mother?" she spat. "You can't exact your vengeance without a proper means to do so."

"*Our* vengeance," Madam Brune corrected. The cubes had all slid together to form a deep amber, and she discarded the empty purses. "But our next step should be to follow our primal duty and destroy those who failed us."

"Did we not just do that, Mother?" Eleanor asked.

"This bastard and his minions inside were the employees of a man who runs an organisation called the Symbicate. The failure of his employees is the failure of him. He must pay for his dishonour."

"It would not be an easy task, Mother. None but the most connected crime syndicates of this land even know who the leader of the Symbicate is," Eleanor said.

"Of course not, which is why we would need to hire a professional to track him down. It would be a high-price job." Her thought was cut off by the approaching of a carriage—a carriage missing a wheel.

"Whoa, whoa!" The driver pulled on the reins, stopping the horses when he noticed the dismembered corpse. "I believe I was here to sell ale to that man," the driver lamented.

"Unfortunately for you, you are too late," Madam Brune said.

The second man hopped off, tall, bald, and pale with a long black leather coat. "But not I! I am here to accept the contract."

"What contract?" Eleanor asked.

"The contract you two were going to put out there."

"We only just thought of that," Eleanor said. She expanded her sword into a shield and circled around the potential threat.

"Calm, my child, calm! This is Luke Sill, a contract killer who has weaved with a living symbioid … it gives you luck, does it not?" Madam Brune asked.

"To a degree—it also prompts me to make lucky decisions," Luke replied. "Like turning up here."

Eleanor retracted the shield and then lowered her blade.

"An amber cube for a deadly task?" Madam Brune tossed the cube between her hands.

"Agreed."

"Excellent, find the leader of the Symbicate and bring him back to me alive so we may exact our vengeance on him … or her!"

"It shall be done."

"Well …" the driver hesitated when they looked at him. "Ah … seeing as I am not needed here, I might just go back the way I came."

"That's lucky," Luke said. He smirked at Eleanor, who looked away bashfully. "Want me to help you balance the carriage back to where you picked me up?"

"Certainly, that would be a great help. I'll even give you a bottle of ale for your trouble."

"Perfect! Madam Brune, I shall return as soon as I have completed my mission—but first, I must prepare myself for a hard task and a long journey."

"Go with honour, Mister Sill."

Luke mounted the carriage, which turned back the way it came.

"An amber cube, Mother? That is costly," Eleanor said through chattering teeth. She regarded the cube in her mother's hands. "This would be the last of our wealth."

"Yes, we will need to recoup our losses. I eyed a hit man's notice board in the tavern there. There was a new official poster offering a rather large sum for a man named Constantine Futruble—dozens of amber cubes for his head, just another Weznin noble who abused his wealth and power. Last sighted heading north past Crankod, and all that is north of Crankod that's worth a damn is Masonville. Eleanor, you will go to Masonville, kill this Constantine, and collect the reward from the bounty guild here. That should shore up our coffers and allow us to strike a blow against the Weznin while Luke does our dirty work against the Symbicate."

"You're finally trusting me with my own assignment, Mother?" Eleanor said.

"I have little choice. I would rather send your brother, but he is tied up in Soth."

Eleanor would have grinded her teeth if not for the fact they were already chattering. "Fine, I'll do it." She made for The Den to find a coat to replace her own before stopping and turning back to her mother. "What will you do?"

"I'll continue our work here to avenge the taking of slaves from our islands … and spread what few cubes we have left to that task until you return. Now go."

Eleanor bowed and stepped inside wordlessly, leaving her mother alone in the bloodied street with the amber cube in one hand and knife in the other.

CHAPTER 5

Thomas Marrow

Boss glanced over his monocle at Thomas. The stout man hadn't set foot in his home city for over a decade and still insisted on wearing the single-eyed invention over a sensible pair of spectacles. He gripped it ever more tightly between his brow and cheek as his gaze flicked between Thomas and the many reports cluttering his desk. His bald, dark umber head shone under the bright gas lamp, which was rigged next to a drafty vent on the low ceiling, like a grim chandelier on a leash.

His head is so shiny, Thomas mused in a weak attempt to rid himself of the feeling of a schoolboy standing before the headmaster.

Snipes sat in the shadowy corner, absentmindedly polishing one of his precision barrel attachments—observing Thomas.

Boss finally sighed and laid his papers against the desk, allowing his monocle to drop and dangle from the chain in his breast pocket.

"Are you aware …" he said with effort, his many years in this part of the world failing to remove the last traces of his thick Mason accent, "of why I might be upset?"

"Boss, I …" Thomas tried to explain himself but was cut off.

"You kicked the client's daughter off a cliff!" Boss rose from his chair to tower over Thomas, or at least he would have—if he weren't so short. "A bloody duchess of Weznin! And you just walloped her over the edge of those ludicrous heights! What in the three perversities are you on, Hooks?"

"She had an aero-break!"

"We had to drag her out of the cold sea, sobbing. My men weren't happy—neither was I," Snipes said coolly.

"A man with hair that red is never happy," Thomas shot at him.

Snipes barged over to Thomas with sinister purpose. "Very original, Hooks, 'cause I have fiery hair, I must be a fiery guy, right?" His Soth accent bled through whenever he got angry, so it bled through quite a lot, at least when he spoke to Thomas.

"Well, you do have a temper!"

"That's it!" Snipes reached for his rifle leaning against the wall—he didn't have to reach far as it was a small office for a small man.

But before Snipes could bring it around, Boss screamed, "I will not have my two best Heroes kill each other!"

"If he was your best, his customer care would be better!" Snipes retorted.

"Says the indiscriminate butcher!" Thomas said.

"You need to let that go, Hooks!" Snipes roared.

"Enough! David, sit down! Thomas, you better have a damn good reason for me to have the duke breathing down my neck, or you're on the street!"

"Boss," Thomas went quiet, "I found a lead."

Boss's expression calmed in an instant. He sat in his chair—only lowering a slight amount. "What kind of lead?"

"One of the men who was there when my father, the Tinkerer, was slain—he was there in the ruins. He was acting on behalf of a man who runs an organisation called the Symbicate … he gave me a location where I can find said man."

"The Symbicate." Snipes whistled.

"You always were gonna make the biggest waves." Boss chuckled. "Where is this said location? Taking out a man like that pro bono would be quite a bit of good press for Hired Heroes."

"Masonville."

"Hah! My old stomping ground, eh? Beautiful place, intricate masonry, if you couldn't guess from the name. Lots of good quality quarries around that place. Heard they've had some troubles since I left though, very tragic. Also very far away …"

"I've been in this for the long haul, Boss. Let me go; let me take my vengeance and earn Hired Heroes some glory in the process. Everybody wins," Thomas pleaded.

"Very well, it'll take you a few weeks to get there, a bit more to track this guy down and kill him, then a return journey." Boss sucked on his teeth. "How about I give you your six weeks' leave, but as a working trip?"

"Sounds good to me."

"Very well, you'll need an advance on your pay then." Boss turned to the wall safe behind him. It was obsidian black with a copper turn dial.

"How will you get there?" Snipes asked. "The highlands between our country and theirs are a desolate place. It'll cost you an arm and a leg to travel around the long way through the main town centres. Crankod would be the closest city by leagues, but even then, you'd have to go out of your way on the next leg of the journey."

"I was going to take my steam tug," Thomas said dismissively.

This got a laugh from Boss as he struggled with the combination. "Ho ho! The Dread Coast, that is a gambit indeed!"

"Why, what's there?" Thomas asked.

"Pirates, for one," Snipes said.

"Pirates crazy enough to sail the Dread Coast for another," Boss added.

"I can handle pirates," Thomas said.

"Then there's the sea life," Boss said.

"Sea life?" Thomas asked.

"Symbioid woven giant squid—can be quite terrifying in the deep," Boss said.

Even Snipes laughed at this. "Ain't no such thing—symbioids don't weave with fish!"

"Oh?" Boss said as the safe clicked open. He eyed the two heroes over his shoulder. His monocle turned his expression even more quizzical. "Have you ever asked a symbioid if that's the case?"

Snipes looked at his feet.

“Didn’t think so.” Boss grabbed a black cube from the safe and tossed it on the desk. “I’m just pulling your leg though, Hooks. You can handle pirates for sure. And sea creatures are a thing to look out for, but the real danger is the shallow rocks along the Dread Coast.” He gripped the sides of the cube with his index finger and thumb and pulled gently, sliding a deep green cube out of the black. He shook his head, “Too much,” and slid it back. He loosened his grip slightly and slid out a cube again, this time a much lighter shade of green, bordering on yellow. “Are you happy with that shade of green for six weeks, Hooks?”

“It’ll do.”

“Good!” Boss pulled the whole green cube out. The black cube—actually a hyper dark red—hardly changed a shade. He tossed the green to Thomas and secured the black cube in the safe again. “All posturing aside, Thomas, good luck. I know what this means to you.”

“Thank you, Boss.”

With that, Thomas left the cramped office, shutting the frosted glass window door behind him. It had black letters etched into it which read “Hired Heroes—Boss.”

“You’re giving him too much leash, Boss,” Snipes said.

“Nonsense, this mission makes it seem like a reprimand dismissal as far as the duke is concerned, which cools his head. And it gives Thomas a little adventure to calm down as well. Now, I do have a job for you; the contract just came in from several city states.”

“At the same time? That never happens.” Snipes leaned in on the desk in interest.

"Well, it seems a wealthy aristocrat has had numerous crimes revealed. I need you to take him out on behalf of the municipalities who can't extradite him from wherever he is hiding. A man by the name of Constantine Futruble."

"Hmm, no word on his location?"

"He bolted some weeks ago, according to the reports from the municipality of Foundton. Lots of fraud and embezzlement, the usual shtick for rich people who have run out of favour ... they want him alive."

"I'll need a few weeks to track him down."

"You have them, but, David ... you won't be the only one after him with the amount of cubes they're offering."

"Understood."

#

Thomas stalked through the tight hallways of the Hired Heroes Headquarters, a revamped ironworks factory, partitioned with wooden walls and concrete floors covered by dusty red carpets. He reached the reception area, another cramped affair, and opened the door, which jingled the bell at the top.

The receptionist shifted awake. "Thomas!" she said.

"Sally," Thomas said.

"When are you going to take me out?"

"I'm busy, Sally, I've got ..."

"Yes, yes." She slumped down onto the desk again, eyes drooping. "You have to avenge your family or some such. The story is always the same; you just don't like me, I think."

Thomas sighed. "Or perhaps you don't like me? I've heard you ask everyone who comes through here if they'll take you out … everyone."

She smirked and closed her eyes. "Can't blame a girl for trying her luck. Have fun on your lifelong quest for vengeance."

"Have fun pestering Heroes and clients."

"Hmph!" she responded as Thomas stepped out into Bronstone Port.

He was hit by the chilly sea air and the cries of gulls in the late afternoon. The sign advertising the Hired Heroes creaked gently. Thomas pulled his maroon cloak closer around him and made for the marina where his ship was moored, his boots tapping over constantly damp stone pavers. The marina was crowded with the returning fishermen for the day—men and women in knitted jumpers with hands calloused to leather marching along the half-rotting wooden planks with their catches of the day. They nodded their respects to the Hero as Thomas marched past them to his steam tug. He sighed, kicked the edge of it in a warm manner, and hopped in. He lit the furnace near the engine and stoked it for a few minutes while adding more coals and then went to the little box that pretended to be a bridge. He gripped the wheel and hit the throttle, and the little boat gently chugged out of the harbour and into the rough seas as the afternoon sun set it alight. As he left the bay, he turned northwards, towards Masonville, towards his vengeance, but first, he would have to brave the Dread Coast.

CHAPTER 6

Tara Night

The Assassin Den was an enigma, an unassuming multi-storied building on one of the busiest intersections in the centre of Copper Cobble—a city built onto a carved flat on top of one of the most mineral-rich mountains in Weznin. The flat almost formed what could be described as an artificial caldera within the mountain's peak, the edges of which hosted the entrances to the many mines that delved throughout the mountain's entire structure.

The Den was a quiet building during the day, boasting a front for muscle hire for various organisations that never seemed to hire their services. The strangest thing about it, however, was the constable's station two blocks away. Everyone knew that the Night Assassins had their headquarters in Copper Cobble, and everyone knew that the Den was that headquarters. But it was also an irrefutable fact that anyone who mentioned this too loudly was not around long enough to mention it a second time.

So it was within this building that Tara stood, behind Billie, who gave her report in the marble-floored suite three-quarters of the way up the building. It had a wide-open balcony looking out to the mountain range that was the edge of the city caldera in the distance.

Despite the shimmering lustre of the icy city in the waning night, the orange glow from the windows and the streetlamps did not do well to illuminate the suite, and neither did the pale green luminescence of the shattered moon.

The Night Mother sat on a large leather couch, the folds of her black robes obscuring all of her features as she swished a glass of red wine in her hand.

Tara felt like a street urchin again in her presence, being scolded by a constable for existing.

The Night Mother stopped swishing her glass as Billie finished her report and placed it on a small table by the couch. She removed her hood, revealing a pale, ageing woman, with greying hair, wrinkled skin, and sparkling eyes … She was smiling.

"Ingenious," she said, her voice warm, motherly … disgusting. It made Tara's skin crawl. "Managing to win his trust and then get him to drink the poison right in front of you! What a way to confirm a hit!" She cackled.

Billie briefly glanced back at Tara, her "told ya so" expression showing even through her goggles.

The Night Mother glided onto her feet and moved past Billie to take Tara's cheek with her hand. "I am actually so proud of you, little Tara." She leaned in and hugged Tara tight. Tara hugged back weakly, trying to suppress the perpetual need to shudder. "However, your skills do need some more refinement by the sounds of it, and your resolve is still in question. So, another test." The Night Mother stepped back, her face now cold, her voice now hard. "In Masonville, there is a man. He is the leader of an organisation called the Symbicate … and his income lately has dried up due to a series of failed kidnapping and smuggling operations, leaving his debts to me unpaid. He knows the price of unpaid debts. I want you to travel to Masonville, find out his identity, and then I want you to kill him. But to prove your skills to me, Tara, I need you to do it face-to-face, with a blade, straight through the heart. If he dies by the hands of another, or in another way, I'll consider you a failure, and I will send your brothers and sisters after you. Understand?"

"The hands of another?"

The Night Mother laughed. "He has made several other criminal rings … upset. I wager he has not got long in this world regardless of our interests, and a contract has been issued to any assassin and hit man worth their salt to kill this man. So do this thing for me, Tara, make an example of this former ally, and earn your place in my family. You have quite a journey ahead of you, on your way, little Tara. And good luck." She tossed Tara a yellow cube. "For your travels."

Tara bowed and turned, leaving the room. Billie watched her go, waiting for the door to click shut behind her. She wiggled her brows, triggering the symbioid woven with the goggles to toggle her lenses, and a red thermal image of Tara appeared on the other side of the door. She was doubled over, breathing heavily.

Billie sighed and turned back to face the Night Mother.

Even if she hadn't toggled the thermal vision, she was quite aware of the dozen other assassins watching from the shadows all around the room. They showed up as red, blurry images, silent on the periphery. The Night Mother was a shade cooler than they were, but that did not surprise Billie. She toggled the image back to normal.

"Is there anything else, Night Mother?"

The Night Mother regarded her with cool intensity. "You place much stock in that one, Billie."

"Her ability speaks for itself."

"Her temperament does not." The Night Mother picked up her glass, downed it in one go, and tossed it over her shoulder to shatter on the marble floor.

Billie suppressed a wince. "She reminds me of me, before I fully surrendered to your will, Mother. She will rival even us if she can just let go of herself."

"Hmm." The Night Mother regarded Billie intently. "Yes, I recall I nearly killed you off for your slow progress many times … and now look at you!" She cackled. "But I have my fears."

"Fears for Tara, Mother?"

"For you. I believe she brings out your past weakness. And I believe she will fail. True, if she overcomes her weakness, she may become an invaluable asset, but if she doesn't, I want you to finish her task … and then finish her."

"Yes, Mother." Billie bowed and made to leave; as she turned, she found a tall assassin looking down at her.

"And Billie …" the Night Mother said, "if you should spare your apprentice if she fails … well … you know what will happen."

"Yes, Mother." Billie eyed the tall assassin before her. "You'll send the Night against us both … and I will kill this one here before any of your blades find their mark." She nodded to the assassin, who grunted a laugh, and she walked around him to leave the room.

CHAPTER 7

Eric Futruble

Eric woke to the peach-coloured high ceilings of his bedroom, lit by the sun piercing through a crack in his curtains. He sighed, smiling to himself, and rolled over to put his arm around Walter, finding an empty space in the red, silk sheets.

"Now, where did he get to?"

The high doors cracked open, and a smartly dressed man with a stiff lip and salt-and-pepper hair strolled in with a tray that held a hot, hearty breakfast and a steaming mug of coffee.

"Good afternoon, Eric," he said, placing the tray down and throwing the curtains open.

Eric groaned and turned from the intense sunlight. "Morning, Daniel ..." He poked his head out from the pillow, his blond hair messy and wild. "Afternoon?"

"Yes, sir. I decided it was time I woke you up."

"Fair enough. Where is Walter?"

"He left a good few hours ago, my boy—had a lot of clean-up work after your exploits last night."

Eric frowned. "That's a bloody shame." He sat up and took a sip from his coffee, sighing gratefully as that first bit of caffeine struck his soul awake.

"I have drawn a bath for you, Eric, if you wanted to enjoy breakfast while soaking away last night's … exertions."

Eric smirked, "Don't mind if I do, Daniel."

He took the tray into the bathroom, where the copper tub was full of warm water and overflowing with foam.

"Ah, Daniel, you do know how to treat a man."

"A pleasure, sir. I have your coat cleaned and pressed as well. Took a while to get the granules of concrete out of it, but it turned out nicely." A bell rang within the estate. "Hmm, I'll go tend to that; you tend to your breakfast and bath." Daniel strolled from the room, and Eric slid into the bath with a groan. The warm water caressed his muscles and skin, which were still aching from blinking so much the night before.

"Ahhh …" He placed the tray over the bathtub, it clicked into place, and he munched on his toast gleefully.

Daniel entered the bathroom again. "Sir, I have an important letter."

"It can wait, Daniel. I'm not decent," Eric joked.

"Sir." Daniel stepped forward and placed the letter on the tray. It was embossed with a golden S, and Eric's name was written in black ink. "I do believe this is serious."

"What seal is that?"

"Sir ..." Daniel sighed, "it's from your uncle. He wouldn't send you a letter with that seal unless the situation was dire. Please just open it."

Eric regarded the butler, usually so obliging but now stern and serious. He ripped open the letter and found a note written with elegant cursive that matched his uncle's.

My Dearest Eric,

How is my nephew doing?

Better than I, I hope, which is the point of this letter.

I have recently received intelligence that my life may be in danger, and from multiple sources, I'm afraid. I don't know who I can trust lately. I am jumping at shadows and keeping one eye over my shoulder. This isn't a way to live, dear boy.

I was wondering if you wouldn't mind giving an old man a visit in Masonville? And if you wouldn't mind escorting him to safety? Do not reply to this letter; it was sent secretly, and your reply might tip off my plans to my enemies.

Travel the untrodden path. I hope to see you soon.

Your loving uncle,

Constantine.

Eric handed the open note to Daniel, who read it quickly. "Should I call for some mercenaries to join you?"

"No, Uncle doesn't know who to trust; mercenaries would be a mistake."

"A fair assumption, sir. I shall get our things ready to leave at once. I have a route in mind that can be considered untrodden."

"You stay here, Daniel. If Uncle is in danger and he escapes Masonville before I arrive, he may send word here again."

"Very good, sir."

Eric sighed, puffing away the bubbles in the bath. "So much for a few days off when the press thought I was out of town, eh? Tell me that route. I'll be leaving within the hour."

"Yes, sir, it's a trail that winds up the Dread Coast …"

CHAPTER 8

The Trio

Thomas relished the kiss of the cool, salty breeze against his stubbled jaw as he stood at the bow of his little steam tug. It chugged away dutifully through the gentle lapping waters of the Dread Coast, which was actually picturesque as far as he was concerned.

Craggy, brownstone cliffs rose up on his left, considerably saner than the cliffs he had scaled to save the duchess. They were riddled with inlets and natural grass pathways cutting along them. A convenience should he have to disembark for any reason. That, of course, was not his plan. He was content to continue his current course until he could pull into the port at Masonville.

He stretched out in the early morning light. The shattered moon was nowhere in sight, which meant a lower tide, he was pretty sure, as imperceptible as it always seemed. Sailors always went on about the tides, but Thomas didn't understand the fuss. Didn't matter once you were already in the water, right?

As he stretched, his maroon cloak billowed out behind him.

Then the boat lurched, striking something beneath the surface of the sea with a spine-shrinking screech.

Thomas lurched with the boat and nearly tumbled over the bronze prow. Halting his plunge into the icy waters by his grip alone, he spun to check on his tiny boat. The bridge—if you could call a small compartment with a wheel and throttle a bridge—stood before him with a plume of smoke behind it from the coal engine. He dashed around the side of the boat and into the bridge to read the gauges.

Nothing read out of the ordinary—he was safe for now.

Another sickening scrape and the boat lurched again; a tear was rendered in the hull beneath the coal fire, beneath the engine. The cold water sputtered against the heated components and gushed steam towards Thomas's little compartment.

"No!" he yelled, shielding his eyes from the hot spray.

His instincts told him that the boat was done for as it started to tilt and sink into the depths, told him that he needed to abandon ship.

The image of a giant squid woven with sinewy symbioids swam past his mind.

"Cogrust!" He scrambled back onto the bow of the ship as it rose into the sky. The sea beneath him boiled and the hot coals sunk ever deeper, consuming Thomas's transport with the inevitable passage of time.

Thomas scanned the horizon—no boats around. The cliffs were maybe a few hundred metres away.

Could I swim a few hundred metres? Could I swim it before anything ate me?

He saw shapes in the water, and his heart rate quickened. His rational mind dismissed them as the tips of craggy corals and rock formations, which he had probably struck. But the primal part of his mind screamed about sea monsters.

"Cogrusted low tide!" he swore.

He balanced on the railing now, the water lapping at his heels. He took a deep breath, preparing for the icy plunge, then raised and fired his grappling mechanism at the closest rock to the shore within range.

His symbioid triggered the mechanism in his forearm, and the grappling hook and tether launched with power and accuracy that would defy physics if it were not woven with a symbioid.

It latched onto the rock.

With another deep breath as his feet began to dip into the cold waters, Thomas retracted the tether and was pulled through the waters.

Cold.

He couldn't even hold his breath—it was so cold. His body went into spasms and he took an involuntary breath half submerged and swallowed what felt like a load of ice into his lungs.

He coughed and spluttered, taking in more water, eyes straining, throat burning despite the chill. He was so distracted he forgot he was being zipped along at a high speed towards a rock formation, and hit it smack on.

His dazed vision worsened, as the cold enveloped him fully now, drowning out all but the gentle thrumming of his heart in his ears, the hum of his constant flowing blood, and a ringing sensation drawing in all around him.

So this is how I die? A moon rock moron who drove into some rocks in cold waters?

There was a flash of sensation—something disturbed the water around him in a flurry of bubbles and friction; then something's limbs enveloped him.

No, I am to die a moon rock moron who went into symbioid-woven squid-infested waters …

An instant later Thomas felt like his body had disintegrated into oblivion. He would have screamed if he had a mouth. The next thing he realised, he was on the rocky shoreline, shivering and coughing and spluttering. His entire body screamed in dizziness and pain.

"Easy there, sailor," a distant voice said. "You'll be all right."

"What the hell?" Thomas screamed through deep gasps of sweet, sweet air. "Why am I hurting all over?"

"I saw you bonk your noggin and start drowning from up the cliff there, so I decided to save you."

"You dove out there from the cliff?" Thomas dragged himself onto his hands and knees in a muddy puddle.

He tried to see his rescuer, but his vision was blurry and he was dizzy from the concussion, the drowning, and whatever black magic had just saved his life.

"No, not at all. I have woven with a conscious symbioid that allows me to blink."

Thomas shot upright, gripping his sword at his side. Visions of his father's symbioid being torn from him by that cruel spherical device raced through his mind. "I'll kill you!"

"Huh?" The blurry figure shifted back, raising his arms.

Thomas drew his blade but lacked the wherewithal to keep his grip on it. It clattered onto the damp ground uselessly. So he drew his knife instead.

"You wouldn't happen to be wearing a golden cloak by any chance, would you?" he asked as he tried to force-squint the blurry figure into focus.

"Do you start all conversations like this?" the figure asked, backing up a bit more and drawing his own weapon.

"My father was murdered by a man wearing a golden cloak, who also robbed him of his living symbioid, a symbioid which gave him the ability to blink."

"Ah." His rescuer lowered his weapon. "Hold your nose closed and try to blow through it as hard as you can. It tends to relieve the dizziness experienced after a first blink, and then you shall see that I am not wearing this cloak you speak of."

"Well, you could have gotten the symbioid from the man who killed my father," Thomas said fearsomely, as fearsomely as he could while trying to implement the man's method for relieving the blink dizziness.

"Not likely. This symbioid has been in my family for generations. It was passed down to me by my uncle."

Thomas's vision swam into focus as he blew his nose, and he could see who he was dealing with: a young man with a strong build, wispy blond hair, athletic features, and a yellow scarf. His coat was not gold, but ornate despite the dampness, pale green with golden trimming and silver buttons.

"And who ..." Thomas said, squaring up against this man's sabre with his long knife and grapple launchers, "are you?"

"Eric." He smiled charmingly. "Eric Futruble. And you are?"

"Marrow, Thomas Marrow." He lowered his knife. "I suppose there must be more than one blinking symbioid in the world."

"By my deductions, there would be dozens if not hundreds. I know people who believe that when the symbioids fell to earth, they were, in fact, a whole being, split by re-entry when the moon shattered."

"A common theory," Thomas sheathed his blade and fished through the damp, rocky mud for his sword, "from an uncommon man. My apologies for threatening you—you saved my life. Thank you."

"A pleasure to help out a fellow adventurer!" Eric sheathed his own blade in a swift motion and grabbed Thomas's hand with a firm grip. "And what is your quest, dear traveller?"

"I am a Hired Hero, headi …"

"Ah, I've heard of that mercenary band. You fellows do fine work for justice."

"Yes … And I'm heading to Masonville on … a personal quest."

"How fortuitous, I'm also heading to Masonville for … well," he smiled, "I guess the same reason."

"That seems fair to me," Thomas said. *Shouldn't expect him to divulge his intentions if I won't.*

"I guess we should become travelling companions. It is still several days' journey to Masonville, and the surrounding highlands are dangerous."

"I … can't think of a reason why we shouldn't," Thomas lamented, remembering the peace and quiet of his steam tug, which was now entombed along the bottom of the Dread Coast.

"Excellent," Eric said, smiling broadly still.

"Would you please stop smiling?"

"No."

"Then would you at least stop shaking my hand?"

Eric glanced down at his firm embrace of Thomas's arm. "So sorry." Eric released his grip. "Shall we hike out of the shadow of this cliff and dry off in the sunlight?"

"I guess we should." Thomas shivered in the chill now that the adrenaline of nearly drowning and fighting to death had worn off.

Eric gestured the way, a narrow trail that ran along the base of the cliff and shoreline and led up onto the peaks. With a sigh, Thomas hugged his coat close around himself, brushed his wet, dark hair from his brow, and marched with a squelching gait.

A few minutes later and halfway up the cliff, the two stopped in their tracks. Clashes of metal and embodied cries of pain rang out from the cliff tops, violent sounds, grunts of a woman and several men in battle. Thomas and Eric locked eyes.

"Sounds like a damsel in distress," Thomas said.

"Seems to be putting up quite a fight, but we should hold all assumptions until we see what is happening," Eric said.

"Again, fair." Thomas shrugged.

"Need a lift?" Eric made to grab Thomas by the waist.

"Whoa, whoa, whoa, no! Hands off! I don't need to feel that dizzy pain again. I'll get my own way up the cliff. Thank you very much." Thomas aimed his grapples up the cliff face.

"A grapple gun? Really?" Eric laughed.

Thomas flexed the symbioid, and the grapples shot out from his gauntlets and latched into the top of the cliff. He retracted them immediately and began running up the wall at speed. All the while mumbling to himself, "Don't look down, don't look down, don't think about it."

Eric raised his brows as Thomas sprinted up the wall with the assistance of his grappling hooks. "Ah, a dead symbioid mechanism, there we go." He focused and blinked up the cliff face, appearing on the edge as Thomas finished his climb.

They locked eyes again, dumbfounded.

There was one woman, lithe, slender, and fighting off four fully grown men on the trail. She wore a close-fitting, brown leather military cloak with a hood and a red scarf, with form-fitting black combat clothes beneath.

"Pirates," Eric muttered.

"Pirates crazy enough to sail the Dread Coast," Thomas added.

"Shall we help?" Eric gestured towards the brawl.

"Does she really need it?" Thomas asked.

The two observed for a moment longer as she was tackled from the rear. Her brown leather hood slipped from her head, and her light brown hair splayed out, catching brilliantly in the sunlight. She spun with the momentum and threw her attacker around her, then jumped in the air and kicked two men on either side of her in the head with a full splits strike.

Form-fitting trousers, Thomas noted.

The fourth man aimed a blunderbuss at her, and she spun, and from the flurry of her coat, a throwing star flung free, lodging in the gun's horned muzzle. The gun clattered to the ground as the man dropped it in surprise and the lady leaped up again, using one of the men on the ground as a springboard to dart through the air and fly kick the gunman in the head.

"So how can you accelerate those grapples so quickly without tearing your arms off?" Eric asked as the lady threw down a smoke bomb and began pummelling the confused men in the haze.

"Dead symbioids aren't really dead … which I'm sure you know," Thomas said as he realised Eric was glancing at him deadpan. "I often have to explain this from scratch, as not everyone I meet out and about is woven with a 'living' symbioid."

"Just a few select mercenaries, I suppose," Eric smirked.

"Well, how often do they congregate? Not very, I would wager."

"Noted, please, continue," Eric gestured.

"Well, I prefer the term 'mechanical' symbioid to dead symbioid. Because they still grow into their mechanisms and circuits. They just have no innate abilities other than a piece of musculature. They grow into the nervous system if woven into a host and given enough time. Mine have had time to integrate into and around my entire skeletal system. When the grapples lift my weight, I am anchored correctly, and my arms remain in their sockets."

"Fascinating," Eric said, as the girl performed a backflip kick and then grappled and broke a pirate's arm without becoming entangled.

"Does your symbioid ever prompt you to take action?" Thomas asked. "That is why they are called living, yes? Not because of the higher abilities but their element of free will?"

"I prefer the term 'conscious' symbioid rather than living; as you said, yours is not exactly dead. Mine has always seemed shy though, hesitant, but it has always served me faithfully."

"Mmm," Thomas mused, "my father's symbioid was always lively, filling him with a sense of mirth and humour."

"Must be nice," Eric said. Thomas glanced at him. "Must have been nice, I mean," Eric corrected.

"I'll never know."

The lady throat-punched a pirate who was going for the gun.

"I really feel like we should help her," Eric prompted again, "for the greater good of fellow travellers."

"Why?" Thomas said. "She ain't no damsel—she will probably resent our help."

"Yeah, but that." Eric pointed out across the highlands, a desolate rocky heath with stretches of grass, crags, stone, and meteoric formations alike. Another group of pirates had surmounted a rise and were charging down to assist their flailing comrades.

Thomas sighed. "After you."

Eric smiled, winked, and then blinked out of existence—he appeared a moment later amongst the charging men, swirling his blade around and causing mayhem, blinking in and out of combat to balance the odds.

Thomas groaned. *You do want to help the little guy … or girl in this case.* He shot his grapple into the fray, looping it around the feet of a man rising behind the lithe lady, and tripped him up.

#

Focus, Tara, you lump of damp coal, focus! Tara rolled over her shoulder and picked up the disabled blunderbuss in a swift motion. She spun on the spot and clobbered another pirate over the head. She was ready to engage the next man when she noticed something odd. Some of them were now fighting each other.

I didn't kick them in the head that hard, she thought.

One—pale-skinned like her and wearing a nice green coat—was engaging several new pirates who were charging over the highland rises—the other, tan olive, in a deep maroon cloak with bronze and copper armour—had swung in with a grappling hook and was tearing things up close to her. To her dismay, they were killing the pirates who, in the newcomers' defence, were already trying to kill her or worse.

Gotta get used to the idea of killing, I guess. She drew the throwing star lodged in the barrel of the gun and flung it at the knee of a pirate behind the hooks guy; the pirate grabbed his knee in agony and doubled over. The hooks guy's tether moved on its own to wrap around one of the men who had broken free of Green Cloak's blinking flurry and flung that man around into another, using him as a crude bludgeon.

While watching this unfold, the pirate behind her rose and went to jam his knife into her back, but the guy in the green cloak blinked into existence beside her and kicked him in the chest, knocking him back onto his arse.

"Thanks," Tara said.

"Don't mention it," the man said, flashing a charming smile despite the fact he was obviously quite woozy.

"That blinking takes a toll, eh?"

"You could say that, miss," the man said, crouching down and holding his side.

Must be winded.

The pirate who tried to stab her scrambled up onto his feet and was now running away. The hooks guy with the maroon cloak had dispatched the last of the pirates around him and was making his way over to Tara and the blinking guy.

"Are you all right, ma'am?" he said.

"My name is not ma'am nor is it miss!" She shot them both a look. "It's Tara Ni ... Nightingale."

"Your name is Ni-nightingale?" The blinking guy panted, his cheeks flushed, and his bright eyes pierced into her soul.

Tara swooned inwardly. "No!" She spun and went to one knee, aiming the blunderbuss at the fleeing pirate, and hoped that the blinking guy didn't see her blush. "Just Nightingale."

"Gotcha, my name is Thomas Marrow, and this guy is Eric Futruble," the hooks guy said.

"Pleasure to meet you." Eric smiled at her; she struggled to focus on the fleeing pirate with that gorgeous face in her periphery.

"Are you going to take the shot?" Thomas said, watching the pirate flee farther away.

"I'm aiming," she said.

"I mean, it's a hard shot, especially with that crude gun at that distance," Thomas said.

"I am quite capable!" Tara snapped.

She aimed down the barrel, sighting the pirate as he fled over the first rise. *Can I really intentionally kill? Even a bastard like that?*

"He's getting away," Eric warned.

"Shut up!" Tara said.

"Exhale before firing," Thomas added.

"I'll exhale before firing at you!" she snapped again.

"Take the shot!" Eric said.

Tara breathed, then aimed away from the pirate before firing. The shot clipped a stone just by his feet. The pirate gasped and stumbled, then picked himself up and tore up the rise of the bleak, grassy heath.

"See, I told you it would be too hard a shot," Thomas said.

Tara gritted her teeth.

"Wanna grapple him back?" Eric asked.

"Too far away, why not blink over there?" Thomas returned.

"Too dizzy, couldn't even fight off a child in this state."

Thomas scanned the several dead bodies that Eric had left behind. "All right, if you say so." *Father's symbioid didn't make him dizzy … at least not after such a short amount of time.*

"Both of you shut it!" Tara screamed, standing and throwing the gun down. "Did it ever cross your misogynistic minds that I might not need saving?"

"Misogynistic?" Eric asked, aghast.

"Hey, you were doing fine, but you were about to be rushed by more pirates. And now that one is gonna get back to his ship and bring his whole crew after us!" Thomas said with raised arms.

"I was trying to find out where their ship was when the banter went sour. I let that guy get away," Tara said. "Look,

I appreciate your help, but I was trying to achieve something worthwhile on my journey."

"What?" Thomas asked.

"I've passed a few farmers out here who have been raided by those pirates recently. I was trying to do a good deed on my way through these parts." Tara crossed her arms and looked away.

"Sounds admirable," Eric said, "and for the greater good. Seeing as those pirates will be coming after us, how's about we stick together on our journey?"

"Where are you headed?" Tara asked.

"We are going to Masonville for … personal reasons," Thomas said.

"Me too." Tara clicked her tongue. "Perhaps it is wise to stick together. We seemed to fight well as a team."

"Mhmm," Eric agreed.

"Now, why are you both soaked?" Tara asked.

Eric and Thomas exchanged glances, and Eric smirked.

"Yes, why are we soaked, dear Thomas?" Eric said.

"That's a long story," Thomas grumbled, "caused by my own stupidity."

"At least you can admit you are stupid then—thought so with that maroon, leather, and bronze colour scheme and those ridiculously bulky gauntlets," Tara chided.

"Hey …" Thomas went to retort but Eric cut him off.

"Hey, his colour scheme is befitting a Hired Hero, and his forearms need that bulk for his mechanisms."

"Sorry, didn't mean to hurt your friend's feelings," Tara said, pulling up her brown leather hood and marching past the two men.

"He's not my friend!" Thomas said.

"Not yet!" Eric cheered as he hauled himself up and marched after Tara.

Thomas cursed under his breath and scanned the highland heath. The first few fragments of the moon were peeking over the horizon, and he could hear the tide drifting in lapping waves down below. *I wonder if it would have been high enough for me to not have sunk if I just waited a few minutes back in Bronstone ... Stupid tides, barely even move with the moon scattered as it is! Wouldn't have mattered!* He pulled his damp cloak tight against a chilly breeze and cursed again. He begrudgingly marched after the two members of his resistant party, leaving the dead pirates to the elements.

CHAPTER 9

The Trio

The band of pirates bustled through the narrow ravine that sat amidst the highland's rock formations along the Dread Coast. They panted foul breath and whined as the captain ushered them on heroically from the front while his first mate whipped them from the rear.

About twenty men, Thomas thought from his vantage point, *not the best odds.*

After a few tense moments, the rumbling of their treading dwindled into a hum, and then was silent. Thomas released a tight breath and lowered himself by unspooling his grappling tether.

He slinked down gracefully like a spider crawling along the first makings of a web—if that spider was sweating profusely. He finally touched ground, and all but collapsed onto the solid comfort of it. He flexed his symbioid to release the latch of the grappling hooks embedded in an overhang at the top of the ravine, which struck Thomas oddly, as the heights made him dizzy, and then the overhanging ravine made him claustrophobic.

While considering the opposing fears, Eric blinked into existence by his side.

"Cogrust!" Thomas swore in a start. "Don't do that to me, man. I'm on edge as it is!"

"I thought that went rather well," Eric said smugly. He looked around. "Where is Tara?"

Thomas waved vaguely to a narrow bottleneck of the ravine behind them. Eric gasped when he found Tara halfway up the ravine with her legs fully split, supporting herself by pressing her feet into each wall.

"They're gone, Tara, you can come down now," Eric called.

"I'm aware of that! I'm just trying to think how to get down," she said.

Thomas spun on her. "You leaped up that rock face quicker than I could grapple, and you can't get down?"

"I was in a rush, okay?" She grunted as she tried to reach for a crag on one side of the wall by her foot. "I could get into this position in a pinch, but it is a lot harder to get out."

"Shall I assist you?" Eric asked.

"You shall not! I'm not some damsel in distress, I'm just … IN stress!"

She reached for the crag, and her far leg slipped, causing her to plummet and scramble for a hold down one wall. She managed to grab a precarious hold halfway down but had scraped her knuckles pretty bad.

"Crap."

She dropped the remaining distance to the ground without incident.

"They came out of nowhere," Thomas said, turning from Tara to track the path of the pirates.

"And they will realise our trail doesn't head down that way sooner or later and double back," Tara said.

"Shall we scale the wall then, head to the farm I saw on foot?" Eric asked.

"I just climbed down!" Tara lamented.

Thomas thought the same lamentation as he looked up the sheer wall again.

"Nonsense, you can get up there in a pinch." Eric winked.

"I still think we shouldn't head towards that farm," Thomas said. "The people in these parts have been harassed enough by these brigands, doesn't seem right to bring a vengeful lot down on their heads. Why not blink up into the skies again and take a look for any other option?"

"That was dangerous enough to do in the first place, Hero. I was dizzy enough from the exertion to almost not see the farm amidst the bleak nothingness of this country—let alone blink back to ground safely," Eric said.

"I do agree with Thomas, though," Tara said. "Why not continue to hug the coast and dodge these guys as we proceed on our respective quests?"

"No," Eric said, his charming grin fading, replaced by a furrowing brow. "We have been playing cat and mouse for days now, and I haven't got many supplies left. Why, I've got ..." he tapped a canteen strapped to some webbing beneath his cloak, "perhaps one day's water left. Without finding a safe place to resupply, we will die out here. I want to safeguard the innocent, my friends, but not at the expense of more innocent. My quest will defend a man who has benefitted countless lives for the better."

"You place one life above another?" Tara asked, trying to check her own judgment as it was—she knew all too well—hypocritical.

"No ..." Eric said shortly. "Yes ... I place the lives one can save over one other life. It may sound harsh, but it is for the greater good."

Thomas cleared his throat yet spoke gruffly. "My father used to say that the greater good is one of the noblest causes to strive toward. Until it isn't. And it isn't when it's at the sheer expense of the individual. Balance, he would say, balance is key."

"We need supplies," Eric said. "Balance won't put water in my canteen."

"Why not raid their ship?" Tara said.

The two looked at her.

"And do you know where their ship is, Tara?" Eric asked.

"No, but instead of being hunted by the pirates, let us stalk them back to their base of operations. There must be an inlet around where their ship is anchored." She spoke quickly, the excitement of raiding the raiders sparking something in her mind.

"How do we stalk them when they are hunting us?" Thomas asked.

"They will need to hunt at least one of us ... for a bit at least, while another follows them, and when their resupply runners peel off to, well, resupply we follow those guys," Tara said.

"So all we need is one of us to be bait and then somehow link back up with said stalker?" Thomas said.

"Exactly!"

"Well, I'm not being bait." Thomas crossed his arms.

"It makes sense for me to do it," Eric groaned, before his smug grin crept back over his face, "for the greater good. I can evade them more swiftly if needed. You two follow them. Since Tara is clearly the more skilled at subterfuge she can follow the men who peel off while you stick with the main party, Thomas. That way she knows where you are, you know where they are, and they know where I am."

"Sounds risky," Thomas said.

"So is dodging pirates around a craggy, coastal moor," Tara said.

"Fine!" Thomas sat down. "Which direction will you take them, Eric?"

Towards the farmhouse to get supplies more quickly, Eric thought. "I'll dance them around these ravines a bit more."

"We have a plan then!" Tara chirped. "I can hear them returning ... you best make a trail away from here, Eric. Thomas and I shall hide."

Moments later, the band of pirates had retraced their steps.

"Where be the cretins?" the captain cried.

"I've picked up the trail of one, Cap'n, but the other two seem to have disappeared!" the tracker said as he crouched over the impressions in the ground.

"How can ye not find the other two?"

"It's a miracle I can find the one, Cap'n, with the footfalls of all of these lumbering wits around." The tracker gestured to the band of pirates.

"A fine job ye be doing then. Would you please lead the way to this lone miscreant?"

"Thataway, Cap'n!" The tracker pointed up the ravine, much to the dismay of the pirates.

"Quit yer belly aching, you dogs!" the first mate taunted from the rear, menacing with his whip.

"Onward," the captain ordered, and the beleaguered force sauntered on with 'encouragement' from the first mate.

Moments later, Thomas lowered himself from his perch yet again, as did Tara—with more grace this time.

"That captain's nice red coat had huge tears down the back," Tara commented.

"Ruffians," Thomas replied.

"Yeah, but the rest of his coat is pristine? Oh well, I'm getting distracted by nothing, I guess. We should hop to it!"

"All right then," Thomas said. "Lead the way, Miss Nightingale."

#

The pirates exited the ravine not too long later and stopped for a quick reprieve. From a distance, behind the strewn moon meteorites that proliferated the landscape, Thomas and Tara could not hear what was being said. But they quickly noticed two pirates peel off from the pack carrying large bags.

"Must be going for supplies," Thomas said.

"Then they are the men I will follow. You stay put, Thomas. Hopefully the rest of the band will do the same." With that, Tara slinked off into the wilderness.

She was gone from all senses before Thomas even realised it.

"That woman must be some sort of ninja," he murmured to himself.

#

Some hours passed, and it was darkening quickly. The shattered moon—flowing imperceptibly across the sky throughout the afternoon—brightened with its pale luminescent green. Eric had been blinking all about the moors in a roundabout way to keep the pirates on track but not enough to catch him, and the constant dizziness was starting to take its toll.

He finally allowed himself to approach the farmhouse and hoped that due to its run-down state that it was, in fact, empty. It was merely a wooden shack, large enough for a small family perhaps, amidst half-tended fields of some pathetic-looking grain. There was no sound of farm animals, no sign of life.

"Those two bleeding hearts. I knew it would be safe to come here." He entered the house via the half-rotten door, which creaked and moaned in protest, and he closed it behind him.

His nose was assailed by a dank, rotted smell, but otherwise, the place seemed clean. It was a single room, scattered with old furniture with a few containers that could store perishables, maybe, with a chimney to one side … and a whole pile of chests against the far wall.

"That's odd," Eric mused.

Curiosity got the better of him, and he strode towards the stack of chests.

The sun dipped below the horizon, turning sunset into dusk and the highland heaths into a bleak, nightmare landscape lit by the pale green of the moon as the red glow of the day faded. The floorboards creaked with Eric's step, triggering a mechanism.

"Well, shit," he said.

One by one, the windows rattled as reinforced iron shutters slammed closed from the inside, and finally a large iron wall shot up by the door, sealing Eric in place. Then the chimney erupted in red, sputtering flames. A flare was shot up from the fireplace, through the chimney and high into the dark skies, exploding in wondrous light.

Thomas started as the darkness was artificially brightened with red light. The group of pirates jeered and hustled from their meagre fire within seconds.

Tara had to crouch behind a tiny rock as the two pirates she was trailing spun on the spot to source the light. One of them chuckled. "Guess our prey finally went to our safe house, eh? Triggered the old booby trap like a right fool!"

"Cap'n's gonna skin them alive! Should we get going to watch the show?"

"Nah, he'll skin us alive if we don't bring back supplies. We can just use the passage between the cove and the safe house anyway, quicker that way. We could actually smoke the rats out. Then the cap'n will reward us for our initiative, methinks."

"You always were smart."

"The smartyest."

"That's not a word, nitwit!"

"Is too!"

The two pirates jabbered on as they continued on their task, and Tara—with gritted teeth at their yammering—stalked onwards. The flare dwindled to darkness, the pale green moon chunks lit the landscape with eerie abandon, and soon the two supply runners crested a craggy outcrop overlooking a cove well hidden by the surrounding rock formations. Within the cove was a masted ship with odd brass contraptions rigged to the stern.

"Sail engine," Tara said curiously.

She waited for the two to descend into the cove—towards a small jetty which jutted out into the waters. After a few moments, they dragged several sacks and a barrel of water off the ship's gantry and onto the jetty. That's when she struck. She leaped from the higher vantage point, drawing two daggers mid-air, and before the pirates knew it, she had landed on top of them, digging the daggers deep into their backs.

They were dead before she had fully driven them into the ground.

She battled the urge to vomit, which redoubled as she drew the blades from the bodies with a sickening wet ringing.

But they were cruel men, and Eric had stubbornly got himself into a spot of bother, and she needed to be swift.

She scanned the darkened cove; the leeward side had a dark depression, which had some rowboats tethered to one side. Past the boats within the cave, she could make out the impression of a tunnel.

"I guess I'm gonna get wet." She took a few deep breaths to prepare herself for the cold and leaped from the jetty.

#

"Crap, crap, crap, Eric, you damp lump of coal," Thomas muttered as he scoured the perimeter that the pirates had set up around the farmhouse, trying to take in weaknesses and blind spots.

Little did he know that within the farmhouse, Eric was saying the same thing. "Crap, crap, crap, Eric, you damp lump of coal." He paced the walls, peeking out between the gaps in the steel shutters, trying to get his bearings of the enemy arrayed against him.

"All right, you cur!" the captain bellowed as he stepped out from the ring of pirates towards the cottage, silhouetted by the torch and lantern light that his crew held aloft. "You caused my men a right bit of damage, and it's time we made you pay!"

A breeze whipped about the area, whipping his red coat around as his crew laughed and jeered.

"Your men were harassing a young woman!" Eric cried from the cottage. "What was done to them was their payment. It wouldn't add up to then make me pay!"

"I suppose that's fair," the captain replied, "but I'm hardly fair now, am I, boys?" The crew jeered and laughed again.

"Could have predicted that answer," Thomas muttered to himself from the darkness outside the ring.

"I walked into that one," Eric said from the darkness within the cottage.

"Now I have a proposal for you, cur," the captain said. "Surrender, and we shall grant you a quick death. Surrender *and* inform on the location of your companions, and I might actually let you live."

"Hard pass, Captain."

"Then you shall die entertaining our boys! I'm a coming for you, worm!" And then the captain collapsed into the dirt, writhing in pain.

Eric and Thomas cocked their heads from their respective positions.

"Captain, Captain, Captain!" the pirates chanted as their leader's writhing intensified.

"Behold!" he cried in agony. "The Angel of Death comes to claim you!"

With that, two monstrous, sinewy limbs spread forth from slits in his coat—gigantic, demon-like wings, with a span as wide as three men are tall.

"Cogrust," Eric whispered. He shifted back as the captain launched himself into the air and arced down onto the cottage roof.

He landed with a crashing clamour and shattered through the roof, trailed by a peculiar figure—Thomas Marrow—who had at the last second barged through the besieging pirates and grappled onto the captain's boot before he launched himself on high.

The captain rose onto his feet, rearing to full height and expanding his wings, drawing his sword to skewer the shocked Eric—right before Thomas sailed in through the open hole in the roof—pulled along by his tether—and crushed the captain flat against the ground.

Collectively the three men released a pained, surprised sound.

"Did you lads see that thing that trailed the cap'n?"

"It was that wretch with the grappling hooks! He must have crushed the cap'n. Open fire, boys!"

The ridiculous trumpeted shots of multiple blunderbusses opened up around the ring of pirates who slowly closed in on the house.

Thomas righted himself just to be tackled down onto the ground by Eric before the walls started splintering from the repeated impacts. Thomas grunted in confused pain before managing to speak under Eric's weight.

"You idiot! You went straight to the farmhouse!"

"No innocents were here! It belongs to the pirates. It's where they hide their loot!" Eric said.

"And we wouldn't be about to be overwhelmed by dozens of angry pirates right now if you hadn't come here!" Thomas groaned.

"We needed supplies immediately, or we were gonna die!" Eric cried.

"And how are we faring right now, Eric? Riddle me that!"

"Piss off!" Eric said.

"You piss off!" Thomas said, shoving Eric from him.

The two took tentative swipes at each other from their prone positions on the floorboards as the walls crumbled around them.

"How about the two of you piss off?" The two froze and homed in on the voice. Beneath the fireplace, Tara creaked open a trapdoor and peeked over the lip, illuminated by the pale green leaking in through the broken roof above. "Are you two seriously having a tiff right before you get stormed by pirates?"

"I guess so ..." Thomas said.

"Well, straighten out your breeches and get over here. There's a way out, towards their ship!"

The first pirate burst through the door—which could be unlocked from the outside—and surged into the room just in time to see the trapdoor click shut.

"They found the tunnel. Get at them!"

Tara led the trio swiftly along the narrow tunnel. The trapdoor swung open and the clattering and muttering of pirates in pursuit echoed along the path. An ominous approaching glow began to overpower Tara's weak oil lantern as they caught up.

"I mean," she puffed as they sprinted, "let's just have an argument instead of running or fighting them off?"

"Hey, it was a rough moment. I was in pain from pile-driving a demon-looking symbioid, okay?" Thomas said.

"About that," Eric said from the rear, "thanks. He had the jump on me."

"They'll get the jump on all of us if you don't shut up and leg it!"

The three burst through the tunnel exit and stumbled into the cold water.

"Cogrust, we're done for!" Thomas floundered in the water.

"The ship, we need to commandeer their ship!" Tara barked.

The two men looked up to the ship mid-splash with the sail engine. They locked eyes and wordlessly formed a plan. Eric blinked up onto the yards and crossbeams on the masts and began the process of unfurling the sails, blinking across the area in order to account for the fact he was one man doing the job of half a dozen.

Thomas grabbed Tara by the waist and grappled towards the helm. He pulled them up out of the water as the pirates spilled out of the tunnel and manned the boats.

"Get on the wheel," Thomas ordered, "and I'll power up the engine!"

"Do you know what you're doing?" she called back dubiously as Thomas fiddled with levers and dials at the rear of the helm, turning large, brass, turbine-like devices to face the unfurling sails.

"It's a basic symbioid mechanism. Once I get it going, it will crank these turbines and jet wind into the sails to propel the ship forward."

"Okay," Tara said, "I never trusted those things."

"Sails?"

"Symbioid mechanisms."

"I grew up around them. Father was a tinkerer—it'll work!"

The turbines whined as they started to spin, catching in the sails with their increasing gale, and the boat lurched, exiting the cove.

"We're away!" Tara yelled.

"Not yet!" Eric warned, pointing down from the mainmast.

On all sides, pirates clambered over the railings of the accelerating ship.

"Cogrust," Thomas yelled. "Propel the boarders!"

"Ye're the bloody boarders!" the first pirate to gain his feet on the deck shouted back.

"I guess that's fair." Tara laughed as she drew her two daggers.

Thomas grappled onto the closest mast to the helm and dropped down onto a group of pirates, beginning to get a foothold on the deck. Tara leaped from the helm to the lower deck, rolling over her shoulder, and came up with a flurry of stabs and swipes at the closest men—taking time to fling out throwing stars when she had the room to do so. Eric blinked down into the fray, dizzy, woozy, but with an enraged flurry from his sabre.

The three fell back under the constant onslaught of the ever-increasing number of pirates and ended up back-to-back in the centre of the deck, murderous eyes closing in on all sides.

"Well," Eric said. "I guess there are worse ways to go."

"I'd rather not die fighting back-to-back with a pretentious viscount," Thomas muttered.

"The pretentiousness is thrust upon me. My greatest regret is that people never saw my true nature."

A pirate leaped in, and Thomas jettisoned him back with a direct shot in the gut with his grapple.

The boat was ushering itself out into the open along the Dread Coast. The dark, still waters glistened with the pale green luminescent light of the shattered moon, which spanned the sky.

Tara thought on her quest, the need to kill in order to help protect those less able, and the fact she might now be letting those people down. Eric thought on his quest to save his uncle, surrounded by enclosing enemies without his help. Thomas on his, the quest for revenge that had consumed his whole life, and he thought on his sister's inevitably short but cruel existence once she was taken from him—he thought on how if he was strong enough, he would have risked anything and anyone to protect her. But here he was, in a makeshift band with two other people who seemed just as clumsy and adventurous as he.

"I guess there are worse ways to go, Eric. I'm sorry I misjudged you. Tara, I'm glad to have met you," Thomas said.

Before Eric and Tara could reply, a loud voice boomed over the waters. "Worse ways to go indeed!" The pirates backed away in momentary fright as something swooped down on them and landed at the helm. It was the captain, the Angel of Death. "And I intend to find a worse way for each of you!"

"He's not dead!" Eric said.

"Yeah, I see that!" Thomas said.

The captain laughed a nasal sound, his innards bruised from the earlier impact, and his nose was undoubtedly broken—but he still smiled down with a charm despite his bloody disposition.

"You think I can be stopped by some hapless imbecile? Lads, gut 'em!"

The pirates rushed in—Tara dropped a smoke bomb.

Thomas and Eric thrashed in the smoky chaos while Tara ducked low and swiped out at knees and ankles around their position, being careful to keep her back in contact with Thomas and Eric so as to not inadvertently attack them. One of the pirates must have dropped his oil lantern because the smoke illuminated suddenly as the oil sputtered, caught alight, and spread throughout the deck—spreading freakishly quickly.

"Spread the fire!" Eric coughed through the smoke.

The trio quickly spread out amongst the confusion and homed in on any oil lantern or torch that they could see in the dissipating haze, killing the confused light bearer and shattering the lantern or tossing the torch at the sails.

"Me ship!" the captain screamed.

He leaped down into the din. With a mighty beat of his batlike wings, the smoke was cleared from the deck—and cursed as many of the flames fanned—and he spotted Tara.

He grabbed her with both hands and hauled her up into the night with a beat of his wings. Her scarf caught on a mast and tore from her.

"Tara!" Thomas cried. He grappled up the mast almost as quickly as the captain took off.

He grappled a second time to reach the crow's nest. With a second beat of his wings, the captain shot past it and into the night sky, becoming silhouetted by the shattered moon. Thomas shot his grapple towards the silhouette. His shot pierced the captain's wing membrane. The captain cried in anguish, and his flight stopped short as Thomas used his other grapple to anchor himself to the crow's nest.

The captain flapped uselessly, tethered to his own ship.

"I don't need to fly higher to kill this one!" He tossed Tara from his grip, into the raging inferno below.

Eric blinked into mid-air, grabbed her, and blinked into the crow's nest with the struggling Thomas.

"Ah, whistling steam that hurts!" Tara grabbed her head.

"Bloody hell," Eric said, steadying himself against the railing.

The captain wrenched the grapple from his wing membrane and was free. He circled around the flaming ship, the single mote of light in the surrounding darkness of the sea, and swooped in for the kill.

"Ah, guys, we need to move!" Thomas cried.

Eric and Tara recovered just in time. Eric blinked away, Tara leaped down from the crow's nest, and Thomas—urged on by sudden need which overrode his fear of heights—dove from the edge, shooting a grappling hook out into the sails just as the captain collided with the nest, shattering it with the impact. The captain shook the splinters from his wings and coat and leaped down into the masts to finish off his prey.

He landed lightly on the mast crossbeam and swung his wing at Tara's legs. She backflipped over the strike and landed a few feet along the beam, preventing the captain from bowling her over. Eric leaped over her crouching form, vying to strike the captain mid-air. The captain brought his wing up like a shield, but Eric blinked just before contact, appearing behind the captain on the other side of the beam and shoulder charging him.

The captain spun as he was knocked from the crossbeam to bash Eric with his wing with a desperate swipe, but Eric blinked away. The captain turned from his fall and made to swoop away and come in for another pass, but Thomas swung in and shot his grapple, piercing his other wing.

Instead of pulling against the tether, the captain swooped tightly around with gritted teeth and made a beeline straight for Thomas. Thomas's eyes widened, as the demon was illuminated by the harsh yellow flames below and baring teeth with a bloody, manic sneer. Tara threw a throwing star which embedded in his side mid-flight. The captain screamed and slammed into the crossbeam, taking it in the gut, and only barely managed to hold on.

Tara flipped forward—landing close—and jammed her knife into the captain's wing, pinning it to the beam. He roared and clambered up onto the beam, trying to wrench his wing free without tearing more of the membrane. He reached over to grab it when Eric blinked in on the other side and impaled the other wing to the beam on his end. The captain was trapped in place; he could now not reach for one wing without tearing at the other.

Seeing his opportunity, Thomas grappled onto the upper beam on the adjacent mast. He accelerated up and shot over it, jettisoning himself into the smoky air. He let his spool slacken as he fell over the other side and then it went taut, sending him swinging down at the perfect angle to kick the immobilised Dread Coast pirate in the chest with both feet.

The impact knocked the wind from Thomas, but it also knocked the captain back, tearing and slicing his wings as they were pulled against the embedded blades. He tumbled into the inferno below. His tattered wings flapped uselessly against the wind as he was engulfed by the flames.

"We don't make a bad team at all," Thomas gasped, righting himself unsteadily as he realised not only that he was up very high, but balanced precariously over a flaming hell.

"Yeah, we managed to stop the pirates, and all it cost us was a terrible death by flames, or hypothermia in the water if we try to swim," Tara said, maintaining her balance much better than the other two.

The boat lurched to a halt, nearly knocking the three from their perch.

"Shallows?" Eric asked.

Thomas looked up, seeing the moon. "It's higher tide ..." he said. "The boat shouldn't be hitting the rocks."

There was a shudder as several giant tentacles rose from the water on each side of the ship and pierced the flaming hull, sending shockwaves and splinters everywhere.

"Giant squid!" Tara screamed.

One of the tentacles split into dozens of different, sinewy strands, which hunted down and plucked surviving pirates from the deck and dragged them beneath the surface with horrified screams.

"Symbioid woven giant squid!" Eric screamed.

"SWiGS?" Tara said in a terrified, surreal state.

"I thought Boss was only pulling my leg," Thomas said in bewilderment. "Eric, you need to blink us to shore, or we're all gonna die."

"I can't!"

"Do it, or we burn or freeze or drown or get eaten by that thing!" Thomas gestured wildly yet needlessly to the terror below.

"Do it, Eric!" Tara urged, snapping from her momentary, surreal panic.

"Okay, okay!"

Eric grabbed the two of them, took a deep breath, and just as three of the tendrils rose to grab them, they were gone.

All they could feel was cold—Eric tried to scream but breathed in icy water. Thomas floundered again, finding himself drowning … again.

But Tara kept her wits. She grabbed the two men and half swam, half towed them to the rocky shoreline which was only feet away. Thomas was still coughing and spluttering, so she plonked him down not too gently and leaned over Eric's still form.

She began compressions, and soon he was coughing and spluttering too.

"Well done, sir," she said, patting his head as he heaved and vomited the ocean onto the rocks.

"You saved me," he wheezed.

"You saved us." She shrugged.

Thomas had calmed somewhat and was watching the burning ship as the SWiGS destroyed and dragged it into the black waters, leaving the water dark again save for the reflected shattered moon.

"And why are you so upset?" Eric wheezed, looking at Thomas's forlorn expression.

"We still need supplies, and now they are burnt, waterlogged, and probably being ingested by God knows what."

The other two sat with him. They huddled together in a vain attempt to find warmth, and steam puffed from their shaky breaths.

"I guess we'll die out here on this heath," Eric said, "on this bloody Dread Coast."

Tara was silent.

"Dread Coast indeed," Thomas said.

"I'm sorry," Eric said, "for rushing in for the quick and risky option. It was selfish."

"And I guess I'm sorry for being overly critical of you when we needed to work together," Thomas said begrudgingly. "I would do the same thing as you to lessen the time between myself and the protection of someone I love, if I still could, I mean. You aren't all bad."

"Neither are you … for a grouchy sap." Eric smiled, teeth chattering.

"So you two have finally made nice?" Tara asked.

"Hardly matters, does it?" Thomas said. "We're gonna starve out here or desiccate or freeze."

"No, we aren't," she said.

"That's optimistic even for me." Eric's laugh quivered.

"There are some supplies on the jetty where the ship was anchored, and I'm sure the farmhouse had some firewood. We'll be fine."

She rose onto her feet and gestured for the two men to follow her, but they looked up at her dumbfounded.

"You could have mentioned that earlier when we both thought we were gonna die out here!" Thomas said.

"What? And miss the opportunity for you two to make nice?" She smirked.

"Well then, I guess we were the damsels in distress this time." Eric nudged Thomas.

"You know," Tara said, "I wouldn't mind it if I was your damsel every once in a while …"

Thomas shifted away slightly, feeling suddenly uncomfortable.

"Oh …" Eric said. "Sorry, Tara, but you aren't my type."

"Don't go for strong women?" Thomas cut in quickly in an attempt to undercut the awkwardness.

"Not at all," Eric said. "I don't go for women in general."

"Oh," Tara said. "Yeah, I could tell that. I was just saying … you know." She turned and strode off towards the cove.

"Tara," Eric called after her, and she stopped mid-stride, itching to keep moving. Eric removed his yellow scarf and handed it to her. "You lost yours on the ship … for saving me."

Tara snatched the scarf, "Thanks," and marched away. *Stupid girl, you don't have time for that sort of stuff anyway. Stupid girl, you have a target to focus on! He obviously wasn't for you.*

Eric sighed and turned to offer Thomas a hand up but hesitated when he noticed Thomas' perplexed face, scanning him up and down.

"Is there a problem?" Eric asked.

"Not at all," Thomas said. "You just struck me as a ladies' man, that's all."

"Like I said," Eric said as he helped Thomas up, "I am often seen differently than I probably really am."

"I'll do what I can to subvert that," Thomas said, "though I do feel like you just broke that poor girl's heart."

"Like you said, Thomas, she is a strong woman. She'll be fine."

"Noted."

The two men took off after Tara to find food, water, and warmth.

CHAPTER 10

Some Other Players

The chilling wind blew against the indomitable stone pavers of the markets of Quartrant. The sun was a rising golden orb that cast the sky into pale blue, endlessly battling to fade the crumbled moon from view. The warmth burned off the light fog that had rolled in overnight, but Billie's breath still misted and mixed into the steam rising from the fresh bread she just purchased. She warmed her fingers on it, leaning up against the edge of the shop as the baker pottered around within, and she staked out the traders through the empty market stalls in the morning light.

She had shadowed Tara all the way down from the peak of Copper Cobble and then as she cut across country to Quartrant—which surprised Billie, as she knew a quicker route from Bronstone Port—before losing sight of Tara in the crowds. This didn't worry Billie so much as she knew there was only one caravan leaving for Masonville within an acceptable time frame. What worried her was that she was staking out this caravan as it packed up to leave on the edge of the city, and Tara was nowhere in sight.

She isn't so good to have given me the slip, Billie mused. *I doubt she even knew I was following her.* She tore into the steaming roll and let the warmth permeate her numb fingers. The scent hit her in full force as she ripped it open, and her mouth salivated.

"This is delicious," she mumbled through half a mouthful.

"Thank-ee, miss." The baker beamed. "Care to buy another one for a white cube?"

A street urchin was weaving through the stalls of the market. "Yes," she answered, "one for my associate here."

Billie tossed a bright cube on the counter and picked up another roll as the ragged child sidled up to her with a sensible sense of false shyness.

"Well?" Billie asked.

"No lady matching your description has spoken to the caravan master, miss."

"Hmm." Billie tossed the roll from one hand to the other. "Where could she have gotten to?"

"If you please, miss. A lady like you said did speak to me just one day earlier."

Billie turned her goggles to stare down at the young boy, who tried to make himself appear smaller. "And why didn't you tell me about this beforehand?"

"Begging your pardon, miss, but you didn't ask … usually better not to offer information freely."

Billie sighed and tossed the roll to the kid, who bit into it ravenously. "Whenever you're ready, boy."

"Hmm," the urchin grunted through mouthfuls, speaking in half gibberish, but Billie got the gist. "She was asking about the same caravan and seemed annoyed by the time it would take to get to Masonville, miss. Said something about walking the Dread Coast."

Billie laughed. "She really does take after me then, hardly likely to survive that." She bit her lip. "All right, boy, run along now."

"Aye, miss!" The urchin scrambled through the market stalls and down a side alley towards Shanty Towers.

Billie stalked towards the Merchant Caravan, formulating a plan. *If she is going by foot along the Dread Coast, she could die … I might not have to kill her at all. The caravan will be a slow trek through the highlands, probably better to backtrack to Bronstone and take a tall ship to the Baul Islands and charter another tall ship to Masonville; that would avoid the pirate-and-squid-infested waters … let's see how much this caravan master wants to extort me before deciding.*

The caravan master was indigenous Weznin, like her, with tanned olive skin. He wore heavy fur coats and had a big hat, a bushy moustache, was short and round, and was adorned with many trinkets and jewellery. The caravan was the busiest part of the market so early in the morning as it was getting ready to set off. It consisted of three steam wagons, bulky carriages on iron caterpillar tracks with overly complicated steam engines set into the front. The drivers were obvious from their grease-smeared overalls and conductor hats, tending to the engines with oil cans and ensuring the water and coal supplies were adequate. Passengers and traders loaded their goods into one wagon and found their seats in the other two.

Billie noted a Soth mercenary, with skin much paler than the new Weznin folk and fiery red hair, clambering into the first wagon, carrying a large case slung over one shoulder. She recognised the maroon coat he wore as a Hired Hero uniform and hesitated. Hired Heroes were among one of the better merc forces in Weznin, but no match for a Night Assassin should a one-on-one fight ensue. Still, it was best not to draw too much attention to herself. She circled around the front of the wagons and decided to watch for a while.

#

Eleanor Brune tugged on her bulky green coat, which was the only coat within the Den from the battle the night before that was not drenched in blood or liquor. It was too big for her though, and it kept slipping off her shoulders, revealing her dress, which was not suited to the cold. As always, her sword-shield poked up over her shoulder and out past her waist, such a big weapon as it was.

She marched through the markets of Quartrant, bubbling into liveliness as the day started, and approached the caravan master on the edge of the town.

"Good morning, sir." She bowed. "I hear you're one of the only caravans heading north for a while?"

The caravan master turned and sagged. "Oh, no, sorry. We are fully booked out. We can't take on any stray that happens to turn up last minute."

Eleanor raised a single eyebrow. "Strays, sir? Or do you have something against Baul Islanders?" She was doing a good job of not grinding her teeth, but realised her fists were trembling.

"I have nothing against Baul Islanders!" He waved his hands. Eleanor saw through his false demeanour. "But you do seem a warrior, and I do have delicate types travelling with us today, not used to such ..." he eyed the sword-shield on her back, "weaponry."

"Then hire me as a guard. You seem lightly armed for such a caravan."

"Why would we need guards?"

"Well, as a Baul Islander warrior, I am well aware of all the ambush locations along the routes in the highlands ... I've used them myself on many caravans like this."

The caravan master's eyes bulged.

"And if any Baul islanders were to see a fellow warrior guarding this caravan, they might decide to hold off on raiding it out of respect." Eleanor's eyes hardened.

The caravan master smiled with his greasy, fake friendliness. "Why not travel with your companions if you know the area so well?"

That stumped Eleanor, especially as she had never travelled through the northern highlands, nor was she aware of any of their freedom fighters raiding the trade routes along it. "Never you mind that. Just pay me a green cube, provide food and shelter for me, and your caravan will be much safer on its journey."

The merchant considered this for a moment. "A blue cube?"

Eleanor narrowed her eyes. "Dark blue."

"Deal!" The merchant pulled out an orange cube from his robe and slid out the appropriate colour. As he handed it to Eleanor he said seriously, "But you travel well out front as a scout, at night you come get your tent and food, and then travel back out. I don't want you interacting with my customers."

Eleanor grinded her teeth. "If you say so." She snatched the cube from his hand and marched towards the front of the caravan by the gate, where she found a black-robed figure leaning against the entrance pillar. She wore goggles and watched Eleanor intently.

"What?" Eleanor snapped.

"Why do you put up with such blatant discrimination?" the robed figure asked.

"I'm used to it in this country."

"Hmm, business in Crankod?"

"No."

"Masonville?" Eleanor didn't answer. "Hmm, that's a shame. Someone of your stature must be after a bounty. I hope it's not my mark."

"If it is, we may come to blows," Eleanor said.

Billie sighed and shifted up, readying herself. "Why wait?"

Eleanor's fingers twitched, ready to reach for her sword-shield, but she took a breath and sighed. "Because I've only just cleaned the blood from my blade, and I'm already on a mission I don't believe in. I'd rather not kill unless I had to."

"But you're a freedom fighter, no?" Billie cocked her head. "Fighting for your people?"

"At the whim of a militant matriarch, I wish there was another way."

Billie sighed. "I suppose I can understand that … What is your name?"

"Eleanor Brune. What's yours?"

"Billie, Billie Nightingale," she answered.

"Hmph," Eleanor laughed, "I knew a Nightingale once. He tried to kill my brother, that was until I skewered him."

Billie smiled, and the lenses on her goggles whirred as they zoomed in on Eleanor's face. "Then I don't think he was a true Nightingale." She stepped away. "But I will take a different route. There's already too much heat in this caravan I think."

"Oh? You afraid you'll meet the same fate as that other assassin?"

"It's just too early for killing," Billie smirked. "I hope I don't see you again."

Eleanor watched her stride out of the gates and into the wilderness of Weznin, feeling a strange mixture of camaraderie and relief.

#

Luke Sill strolled through the damp streets with spring in his step. Towards the caravans on the edge of town, preparing to go on their merchant journeys throughout Weznin, he halted when the tingling sensation down his spine flared.

He turned to the squat and round merchant in heavy furs with a bushy moustache and asked him where he was heading.

"Crankod," the merchant replied. "Heading that way as well, my fine fellow? You seem a man out for a walkabout, a wandering adventurer through and through?"

"Crankod is a bit in the middle of nowhere, unless you want to journey downriver into the Dread Coast." Luke bit his lip, wondering why a man with a bounty on his head would hole up in such an inescapable place—he didn't want to question the luck symbioid though.

The merchant must have taken his confusion for someone about to back out of a transaction. "But ah, the convoy will be passing through Crankod and onto the lands north of Weznin after that, sir, if you don't mind a longer journey, and we will have protection. I have hired the most fearsome Baul Islander bodyguard." He wrung his hands.

"Lands up north?"

"Yes, sir, Masonville, and even beyond to Chepton and ..." Luke's tingling flared at the mention of Masonville. "And to entice you further," the merchant leaned in and looked around, "I can give you a cushioned seat on the wagon for the regular price."

Luke's grin widened. "My lucky day then."

Luke slid out a few pale green cubes from his stash and clambered into the back of the wagon, nodding politely at the crammed-in passengers as he made his way to the end where the cushioned seat was, next to a maroon-cloaked mercenary. He had hyper-pale skin, fiery red hair, and a large case leaning against the wagon wall next to him.

"Morning!" Luke beamed as he sighed and slouched down.

"Hmph," the bounty hunter replied.

They rumbled and swayed as the caravan master called the journey to start. The engines powering the carriages squealed to life with whistling steam, which was compressed and turned into a hiss as the carriages pushed off, hydraulics turning gears to push the caterpillar tracks along. They trundled along the cobblestone path and out of Quartrant into the uneven wilderness.

"Not a morning person, eh? Maroon cloak … you're one of those Heroes for Hire, aren't you?" Luke had to raise his voice to be heard over the steam engines.

"Hired Hero," the mercenary mumbled, revealing a Soth accent.

"Same difference, we'll be cushion buddies by the looks of it. Name's Luke."

"David," the Hero said. "Just call me Snipes, though."

"Interesting name. Those are some nice pistols you've got there." Luke gestured to the two pistols on Snipes's hip holsters. "They seem … different."

"I commissioned a tinkerer to add a revolving mechanism to them. They can fire a whole six shots before needing to reload."

"I wouldn't mind one myself," Luke whistled.

"Well, unfortunately, these are the only ones in existence."

Luke felt the tingling sensation burning throughout his spine. He would get those pistols; all he had to do was wait. "You after a hit?"

"Heroes don't do hits, officially. I'm after some rich guy who's embezzled cubes and is wanted by almost every authority."

"Good thing we won't be competing for the cubes then. Your man is hiding out in Crankod?"

"Last sightings of him suggest he fled through Crankod. Not really anywhere to go from there except further north.

I was going to putter around the Jaunt Saloon at Crankod and see if anyone noticed anything."

"Sounds like a fine plan. I'm heading to Masonville meself."

Snipes raised an eyebrow at this. "I've got a mate—well, a colleague really—travelling that way as we speak."

"What's he after?"

"Some old revenge score."

"And why isn't he taking a caravan like me?"

Snipes's grumbling demeanour cracked. "Took a tugboat up the coast."

Luke cackled. "Up the Dread Coast?! Man's mad!"

Snipes laughed too. "Knowing him, he's probably already there safe and sound."

CHAPTER 11

The Trio

The trio trudged a sodden uphill path, marked with ditches and stone.

Grey skies and drizzle bore down on the heath, punctuated by shrubbery and a solitary, decrepit tower on a rise with windmill-like arms that bent and jutted out at awkward intervals. Cold coastal air swept over the hills that separated the ocean from the path of two content adventurers and one disgruntled nobleman. Eric sighed when he snagged his worn boot on yet another exposed root embedded in the muddy path. With a wet plop, he slumped down to the ground and crossed his arms.

"These are abhorrent conditions for an adventure!" he said.

Ahead, Tara and Thomas exchanged looks. Thomas pulled a timepiece from his coat pocket and groaned. "Cogrusted Ninja! I thought he would last at least another day."

"Pay up, mercenary man!" Tara chided, nudging Thomas not too gently in the ribs with her elbow.

"Excuse me!" Eric cut in. "Have I lost my mind or have you two placed a wager on my misfortune?!"

"It's not only your misfortune, Viscount," Thomas said. "We all share in the wonders of this adventure."

"Pay up!" Tara swiped at Thomas playfully. He ducked under her blow while offering a placating gesture as he reached into his coat.

"Wonders?" Eric stood up, slipped slightly in the mud, and marched up to the two, his angry demeanour nullified by the wet plopping of his boots with each aggressive step. "This drizzle is more disheartening than a torrential downpour! I keep tripping on filth, and the cold air is starting to disquiet my sensibilities!"

"And that," Thomas slid a medium shade blue cube from the darker cube in the shadows of his robe, "is what adventure is all about. Braving the elements as a team, the perseverance that many omit from the tales."

"Did you think an adventure was all swashbuckling and pirate slaying?" Tara chided as she snatched the cube from Thomas and slid it into the cube within her own jacket.

"No! I've had adventures before. Do you think it's a quick affair to track down smugglers and break up criminal rings?" Eric protested.

"A damn sight quicker than marching across the Dread Coast," Thomas said. "Cheer up, Eric, isn't this what you wanted, for all of us to bond over adversity?"

Eric narrowed his eyes at Thomas.

"I figured so," Thomas said with a smirk. "Now flash us that unbearably charming smile and let's soldier on over the next rise; then we can find some shelter at that abandoned signalling tower and grab a bit of rest, eh?" Thomas clapped him over the shoulder and continued up the rise.

"Cheer up, Eric," Tara said. "We'll be there soon."

"I feel like we've been marching for years; soon may not be soon enough," Eric grumbled as he trudged past her.

"Nonsense, we'll get to Masonville. You'll find this powerful friend you keep not talking about and get to soak your feet in a nice hot foot spa!"

Eric groaned, imagining the sweet relief. "And where will your quest take you, Tara? Perhaps you can come over to our estate and enjoy a spa yourself?"

"I have my own business to attend to, Viscount." She drifted off as they crested the rise where Thomas had halted. "Why is that signalling station abandoned?"

"It must be the Masonville messaging tower—we really are close. They don't like relying on symbioids for 'trivial' things," Eric explained.

"Finally. I thought everyone and their dog had a symbioid at this point. Aren't people woven with symbioids supposed to be few and far between?" Tara asked.

"I guess so," Eric replied, "but in our line of work, we are more likely to come across them."

Tara hummed in thought. "So they tore out the symbioid woven into the signalling limbs of the tower?"

"Likely, they just left it in there. Not like it's going to go anywhere, is it?"

Tara was silent as they caught up with Thomas, observing the signal tower, which stood alone upon the heath. Its many multi-jointed windmill-like arms were still like some surreal structure. "Sad really," she finally said. "Is that why Masonville seems so isolated?"

"Indeed, but it's not like they're cut off from the world entirely. They …" He trailed off as he caught up with Thomas too and halted, looking out over the vista.

"Behold," Thomas said quietly, "Masonville."

Before them, the highland moors of the Dread Coast flattened into a prairie, and across the vast distance from them, the city sprawled.

Masonville.

It had walls of enormous white clay bricks, and the infrastructure within seemed to be carved entirely from the same material. Within the windows, there were glints of the many colours of stained glass, and upon the spires was the ever-prevailing shimmer of bronze and silver capstones in the grey, veiled light amongst the city sprawl. It sat on the edge of the prairie and connected with the sea, and at the port, there was a constant stream of boats and ships moving to-and-fro.

Across the prairie, there were roads of traffic, travellers, and traders spreading out from the city like the spokes of an intricate spider's web, leaving trails of steam from the steam wagons that trundled along the paths.

"It's beautiful," Tara said.

"It's enormous," Thomas lamented.

"It was my childhood home." Eric beamed.

Slowly, the two swivelled their necks to look at him.

"Then why such anguish on our journey, if you knew the way so well?" Thomas asked.

"I never came this way, never alone, and I have not been back since I was but a child," Eric answered.

"That explains why you know a bit about it. But why did you leave?" Tara asked.

"My parents died when I was quite young … my uncle took me in. He said people within the city were trying to seize my family's estate while the heir—me—was still vulnerable, so he fled the city with me. He must be in dire straits to return to Masonville now."

"I'm sorry," Thomas said.

Tara coughed. "Shall we?" She gestured to the descent into the prairie, to join up with a trafficked road at the base of the rise.

"We shall," Eric said, shaking the nostalgia away.

The trio descended and quickly enveloped themselves into the diverse crowd. It was travelled by peoples from all different parts of the world, wearing blends of sensible travelling clothes or exotic robes. Some few were lucky enough to ride on steam wagon or horseback, trailing carts and supplies.

"What the hell are those?" Thomas pointed across the plain to another road converging on a fork on their path.

"Elephants!" Tara squealed.

The lumbering beasts trod steadily across the prairie, trailing a gargantuan cart behind them which caused the earth to rumble beneath the feet of the trio still so far away.

"What are they hauling?" Thomas asked.

"Stone from the quarries to the west," Eric said. "Those beasts are the only ones strong enough to haul the sheer amount of materials that Masonville extracts from the earth."

"So they are glorified mules?" Thomas asked.

"Not at all, quite intelligent animals. They are treated better than any other animal in this country due to how valuable they are," Eric said.

Thomas looked to Tara, who had run ahead on the path to the fork, jumping up and down on the spot as the huge beasts converged onto their road.

"Well treated or not, they spend most of their time hauling things ... not a way to live," Thomas said.

"A sacrifice for the greater good. It's not like they're slaves, Thomas. Why, if we left them to wander these lands untamed, they may be hunted into extinction."

"Become a mule, or die," Thomas said quietly to himself. "Poor things ... And where do all of these people hail from?"

"All over. Masonville isn't the only city on this side of the highlands, you know."

"Fair enough," Thomas said.

They marched on in silence as Tara dashed along the trade route, marvelling at the many different things. Over the course of the day, the skies began to clear as the drizzle was blown inland by a gentle breeze. Eric perked up despite the constant chill.

"We're getting closer," he said. "I can see the gates from here."

The road they took grew packed as the flow of travellers was stemmed by the bottleneck at the gate.

"Strange," Tara said, "their guards walk around in pairs, but only one carries a weapon, a giant pike ... so odd."

"Ah," Eric exclaimed, "that is where the Masons have a great advantage over this prairie. Those pikes are long guns. Do you see how the guards without pikes have those strange little nooks in their shoulder plates?" He pointed to one as they passed him. Tara nodded.

Eric continued, "When firing, the guard with those shoulder plates takes a knee, and the barrel of those long guns rest in that nook. They stabilise the shot essentially and help the gunman swivel and aim. They fire smaller shots, less damage to the barrel that way so they can keep them narrow. And because the barrel is so long and doesn't trumpet out like most blunderbusses, they can fire extremely accurately over long distances."

"I know a guy who made his own attachments for his blunderbuss. Narrows the barrel, but they burn out after a few shots … we call him Snipes," Thomas said.

"Sounds like a smart guy," Tara mused. "That sounds much more manoeuvrable than these long guns."

"He's an asshole," Thomas said.

"A manoeuvrable asshole," Eric joked. "But mobility isn't the strength of these guns, Tara. Imagine you were an army charging across these plains, straight into a phalanx of hundreds of those long guns; then once you get close enough, you'd have to impale yourselves on the vicious-looking bayonets they sport."

Tara glanced up the barrel of one of the long guns—three times as long as she was tall—and grimaced.

"Eric, are the customs usually this bad?" Thomas asked as the trio halted in line to get into the gates.

"Not as far as I remember, but I have heard reports that a lot of miscreants are being let in lately. They've had troubles, you see. Oh, and they don't like symbioids too much, like I said. They have one exception to this distaste; they have to be for use in some grand quest."

"As judged by who?" Tara asked.

"The customs officer, of course."

"Why don't they like symbioids?" Thomas asked.

"Some troubles they had about a decade ago. Did you see from our vantage point in the highlands how one section of the city had no coal or chimney smoke?"

"I did."

"Apparently, some symbioids went rampant right before we moved away, taking over their hosts and nearly the entire city … then they just stopped. They keep that section quarantined."

"Then why allow symbioids in at all?" Thomas asked, inspecting his gauntlet launchers closely, having never felt his symbioid fail to respond to his commands, let alone take over his very body. It was an unnerving thought.

"Why, it's in their culture, they know symbioids can be tools for heroes, and they love a good adventure!" Eric answered.

"Things about you are starting to make sense," Thomas murmured.

"So what if they don't let you two in?" Tara asked.

"We'll just have to hope that our quests are up to their standard," Thomas answered.

After a time, the trio moved closer in line towards the gates and were called through one at a time through a customs' checkpoint. The officer was a tall man. His burnt-umber skin—characteristic of the people of Masonville—was shiny as if oiled, and his broad smile rivalled that of even Eric's.

"Greetings and welcome to Masonville, traveller!" he said to each of them in his thick Mason accent. "You seem as if you are a great adventurer. What manner of quest brings you to my city?"

They answered in turn.

"Revenge," Thomas.

"Duty," Eric.

"Survival," Tara.

"Ah," the customs officer said in response to each of them. "A fine quest indeed. Please enter. But be warned, while we encourage you to pursue your goals, the breaking of our laws will not be tolerated."

Within the walls was a great bazaar that spread throughout the clustered streets. The three met up just inside.

"Well," Thomas said, "that was easy."

"Mmm, too easy," Eric said as he took in the manner of the crowds around them.

Thomas and Tara followed his gaze and the realisation dawned on them. Every other person seemed to be some sort of mercenary or adventurer. Warriors walked around in loud groups carrying those crude blunderbusses or stuck to pairs or as lone wolves who stalked about, scanning the area for whatever it was that they were searching for.

"It seems as though Masonville is a hot spot for quests at the moment," Tara said. "I wonder what could have caused this."

"Well, I've seen no less than ten wanted posters for this fellow, and we haven't even been here for five minutes." Thomas gestured to a notice board in the bazaar.

"*WANTED*" it said in large bold ink. "*Dead*"

"*Known as: RELLA*"

Below these lines was the rough sketch of a man dressed in a dapper suit, coattails, and a large top hat, which shadowed the face but not the monocle and broad, bushy moustache which protruded well from his cheeks.

Beneath the crude sketch it read. "*Crimes: Sympathiser and champion of the Symbioid Zombies*"

"*Reward: Dark Amber Cube*"

"*Caution, extremely dangerous*"

"That is a hefty reward," Thomas mused.

"Is that why the Hired Heroes sent you to Masonville, Thomas, to get a piece of that action?" Eric asked.

"No, I am here on personal quest leave," Thomas said.

"That sounds made up." Tara laughed.

"It's all the rage with professional mercenaries these days," he joked back. He thought on it, and added, "I'm here to avenge my family. My father was killed when I was young, and my sister was taken from me to die ... I am here to find those responsible."

"The man in the gold cloak?" Eric asked.

Thomas nodded.

"I'm so sorry," Eric said.

"Me too," Tara added.

"Well," Eric said, "whatever the quest, whether it be revenge or," he waved at Tara, "whatever it is you're doing, they seem just as pressing as mine. I believe this is where we say goodbye."

Thomas extended his hand to Eric. "Goodbye, Viscount. I'm surprised that I'm happy to say that I can now call a nobleman friend."

Eric took Thomas's hand with his own strong grip and shook enthusiastically, just enough to make Thomas feel uncomfortable again, which he smiled at.

"And I'm glad to count such a resourceful man as you as one of my dear friends."

Once they released their handshake, Tara hopped in and embraced Eric tightly. "You take care of yourself, Eric, don't go getting yourself into trouble again!"

Eric returned her tight embrace, picking her up from the stone ground so that her toes scraped against it gingerly. "You take care too, you little ninja. Don't go getting yourself into hard-to-reach places without an exit strategy, hmm?" Tara laughed as he placed her down. He stood back, taking the two in, and sighed. "Well then, good day to you both." He gave a tiny salute with two fingers and strode off into the bustling crowds.

"Hmph," Thomas laughed, "even with that ridiculous coat, he still blended into those crowds seamlessly."

"You just aren't looking well enough." Tara nudged him. "I suppose we have to go our separate ways too."

"So it seems." Thomas leaned in and hugged her gently. "You know, you remind me of my sister, Sybilla. She was rash and foolhardy just like you."

Tara leaned back from the embrace and glared at him.

"And like me ..." Thomas concluded.

Tara smirked and hugged him tighter. "I'm sorry you lost her, Thomas. You struck me as what I imagined a proper big brother should be like. Cranky and rude ..." Thomas laughed. "But hiding a sweetness about you. Don't let it hide too long, eh?"

"I will hide it until my task is done; then I will have no reason to protect it," Thomas said.

"Come find me—if we both still live after—come find me in Copper Cobble."

"That's the peak near Bronstone Port, where Hired Heroes is based. I'll come find you, little ninja."

She stepped back from his embrace, and with a sad smile, he turned from her and walked into the crowds.

"Now his cloak does blend in a lot more than the viscount's," she mused to herself.

She turned to take her own path down the bazaar streets, dodging salesmen and merchants and pickpockets, all trying to extract something from her, until she came to an opening, a plaza in the bazaar.

Where to begin? she thought, as the magnitude of the city began to hit home.

Her thoughts were distracted by a commotion within the plaza. She slinked into the shadows beneath a merchant's stall and observed.

"So you're the mighty Regen, huh? Not much to look at, are you? You are a long way from home."

Tara's mind raced. *Regen? The most famous assassin from Estaka, the land across the sea?*

She homed in on the challenge, and a clearing formed as the common folk stepped back—as if from some minor inconvenience. This was probably the umpteenth time they had witnessed these adventure types clash in the street.

One man stood out against four surrounding challengers. He was wearing eastern robes and leather banded armour with a wide-brimmed conical hat that had armoured plates studded onto its surface. At his side were two curved blades. Not curved like the cutlass and sabre that Eric and Thomas carried, and the handles were slightly curved too, wrapped with fine silks.

One of the men shoved Regen, but other than a slight stumble, he made no move.

"Are you here for the bounty too? Do you think you on your own can take it from all of us?" The ringleader gestured to his group. "Even if half of the stories about you are true, you still can't hope to beat all of us."

"Fools," Tara whispered under her breath. She had heard the stories. Many Night Assassins had fallen to him when competing for a mark. He possessed a powerful symbioid, one that allowed him to regenerate any wound, hence his not at all creative nickname.

"I am here for one man." Regen spoke with a slow, low voice with a thick, rounded accent. "No more than one needs die, lest more than one halts my path."

"Perhaps that one man is you!" one of the challengers behind Regen cried. He stepped forward and drove his spear through Regen's back.

The remaining onlookers screamed and ran for the side streets. The plaza cleared in seconds. Regen looked down at the spear head protruding through his gut and grabbed it with both hands as his blood leaked down onto the white stone street.

"Not so tough after all!" the ringleader said.

Tara stepped forward to help Regen. He may have been an enemy of the Night Assassins, but that didn't mean she wanted him to die—at the very least, it made her like the guy. She had barely taken a step when Regen reacted. Quicker than a blink of the eye, he drew one of the blades at his side and whipped it over behind his head. The spearman let go and stumbled awkwardly to the side.

"Bruce, what's the matter? He didn't hit you. There's no blood," one of his companions said.

The spearman turned to face his companions as a thin red line spread across his neck; then, to their horror, his head slid off and toppled to the ground. The headless body crumpled.

The three remaining men looked on in shock, as Regen whirled his blade around and slashed the spear head protruding from his gut, severing it. As it clattered to the ground, he reached behind him and pulled the spear shaft from his back with a pained grunt. Blood spurt from the openings on either side of him but it quickly stemmed as his symbioid went to work, using its sinewy tissue to repair his bone, organs, and flesh with its own.

Regen drew his other blade and cut the straps of his broken armour, letting it clatter to the ground in the pool of his own blood. He tore the blood-soaked robe from his body and threw it down, leaving only his trousers, his conical hat, and his lean body. It rippled with muscles and the extensive white tissue that marked every wound his symbioid had ever healed.

"You had much time to leave. Now you have little time to live."

Regen leaped forward with a flurry of strokes and moved through the three men in an instant. After his last swipe he paused on the other side of them and shook the blood from his blades. He stood straight and re-sheathed them as he turned.

The three men turned to face him and made a move to attack, but then fell in three dismembered piles as their bodies caught up with the fact that Regen's blades had slashed right through them.

"Amazing," Tara mused. She stepped out to go talk to Regen, but the atrium was soon filled with dozens of Mason guards, their long, oblong headpieces making them look like something from another world, and they surrounded Regen.

"Please, miss," one of them said to her, "vacate the area for your own safety."

"Yes, sir," she said as she made for a street that was in earshot of the new confrontation taking place.

"What is the meaning of this?" the captain of the Guard asked.

"I merely defended my life," Regen said calmly.

"Very well, we will corroborate your story."

"It's true," one of the stall merchants shouted. "He was attacked first, so he slaughtered the lot of them!"

"In that case, it seems that the men to be punished have already been so. You may leave, sir, and please, find yourself some clothes."

Tara heard no more as she strolled farther down the street away from the atrium. "A hotspot for mercenary activity indeed. If he is here for the head of the Symbicate, then I better hurry, or the Night Mother will kill me dead!"

CHAPTER 12

Thomas Marrow

Thomas spent half the day wandering through the tightly packed streets of Masonville. Above the walkways, there were skywalks and enclosed bridges connecting different levels of different buildings, crisscrossing above ground level.

"This place is a playground for my hooks."

He tried not to dwell on leaving his company of the past weeks. He had a mission—a vengeance pact—to honour, and he was beginning to get fed up.

"Where the hell is the merc contact?" he muttered, turning onto another street in an area of the city that was infested with taverns and pubs alike.

He stopped in his tracks when he heard a tune from down the next lane, a jaunty, rip-roaring melody that stood out from the eclectic mix of songs from different cultures that were being performed in the venues all around.

"That tune ..." he murmured as he followed his ears, "it must be from the Jaunt Saloon."

He trusted his gut and eagerly wove through the ever-entangled lanes and alleys and streets, straining his ears to sense if he was getting closer to the tune amidst the cacophony of others. The Jaunt Saloon was what one might call a franchise spread throughout different cities on the continent, used by a corporation of information brokers who catered to the more adventurous professions. Essentially, the Jaunt Saloon was a beacon for mercenaries, thieves, bounty hunters, and assassins alike to find information on their local targets—for a price.

And Thomas had just located one.

He was sure he was getting closer; he turned a corner and stumbled upon the shanty-esque building. It was squashed, bulging out on the corner from under a complex of units built onto its roof. It sagged outwards along with the drunkard men and women who frolicked and lolled about with their flagons, jeering merrily and singing along with the jaunty piano tune that always seemed to accommodate such a place.

As he approached the saloon, he noticed that many of the patrons were armed to the teeth, save for the bar staff, who wandered around in frilly gowns or tunics—not Mason attire, but it fit the profile of the joint. This place was certainly a hotbed of activity lately. Thomas reached the slatted, swinging saloon doors and placed his hand to push them when a young woman burst outwards and smacked right into him.

The two fell in a heap at the door, followed by friendly, mocking jeers from the merry patrons.

"Don't you know to look where you're going?" she raged as she struggled off Thomas to stand and hesitated when she managed to get a good look at him.

"Don't you know not to burst through swinging doors like that?" Thomas started back, but stopped.

They locked eyes.

*She's gorgeous, h*e almost said aloud.

How handsome, she thought to herself.

She had deep brown skin, a shade lighter than the locals of Masonville, and big brown eyes with long, glossy dark hair, like that of those who hail from the Baul Islands. She wore a form-fitting, powder-blue dress with tactical splits at her legs and a green fur coat for the cold—which Thomas figured as an Islander she was not used to. Also—Thomas noted eventually—strapped to her back was a monstrously big cogrusting sword.

They noticed they were each staring and shifted back.

"I, uh … I'm sorry about that, miss," Thomas said.

"Don't *miss* me. My name is Eleanor," she said.

"Oh, I'm sorry, I'm Thomas." He extended his hand to shake hers but pulled back hesitantly. "I really am sorry, Eleanor."

She relaxed and shot him a half smile. "Not at all, Thomas. I was in a rush to get out of that place."

"Broker's price too high?" Thomas asked.

She snapped him a look. "What?"

"Well, I assume you're looking for some sort of information, on a mark or something?"

She sighed. "You're the first man in this wretched bar who hasn't assumed I'm some silly girl playing at adventurer."

"Ah, well ... technically, I'm not in this bar yet ... I guess I can blame you for that."

She actually chuckled, Thomas felt as if he could fly.

"Well, be careful in there, Thomas. The broker charged me a fair price but some ruffians might grab at your ass."

"This is something I constantly struggle with. Thanks for the warning," he replied.

She chuckled again. "Take care, adventurer." She strode off onto the street, looking back one last time before she turned the corner—to catch Thomas still staring after her.

She smiled again and walked from sight.

"Blimey," Thomas said, before turning back to the swinging doors and entering the saloon.

He was assailed by the dense scent of booze and sweat. His ears were besieged by the riotous laughter, the yelling of some obscure arguments on the far side of the saloon, and by the persistent jaunty piano tune ringing from a player piano on repeat by the stairs.

There was some tall, bald man in a dark military coat causing the ruckus between two tables of patrons, a girl on each of his arms.

Thomas felt a small slice of familiarity in this strange town.

He walked about the room in search of the broker, not quite knowing how he would identify him until he saw a friendly face.

"Charlie?" he called.

"Hooks?" A squat, sun-burned red man with a receding hairline and a white suit looked up from his ledger in a booth.

"Charlie, you fat bastard! What the hell are you doing in this forsaken town?"

"Business, my dear boy!" Charlie stood, but his belly hit the table, so he was knocked back down into his booth chair. "Ah … let him pass, boys. I owe him one after a gig in Foundton," he said to two serious-looking bouncers in military coats on either side of the booth.

They stepped aside and let Thomas sidle into the booth across from Charlie.

"Business, you say?" Thomas asked, as a barwoman with a questionable amount of bare cleavage walked up and put down two flagons of ale.

"Aye, Masonville at the moment is swarming with all manner of hired thugs. As you can see." He gestured around the crammed saloon.

"Hired thugs?" Thomas raised an eyebrow.

"Don't jam my gears, Hooks, I've had a busy day."

"Must be tough being the monopoly of information trade in this city," Thomas said.

"Aye, a tough job." Charlie eyed the passing barwoman as she made more rounds. "But it has its perks."

"I'm sure," Thomas managed to say.

"Now, as for why you're here—I'm not sure. I thought that there was already a Hired Hero in these parts?" Charlie said.

Thomas leaned in. "Who?"

Charlie had already flopped open an enormous tome on the table and was scanning through a list of names using a pair of spectacles that were supported on the end of a long handle.

"Let me see here, hmmm, Frogman." Charlie looked up. "Friend of yours?"

Thomas slammed his fist on the table. "Frogman! That insolent bastard is no Hired Hero!"

"I guess not then." Charlie laughed awkwardly. "What is he then, ah ..." He scanned across the row in the tome. "Ah, a Rent-a-Saviour ... What a bunch of wankers."

"You're telling me. Rent-a-Saviours are a poor man's Hired Hero. But Frogman has snaked a dozen of my bounties and rescues, nearly killed me a few times too," Thomas fumed. "Bloody discount outfit those bastards are."

"I'm sure you've returned the favour though, yeah?" Charlie returned.

"Oh, not as much as I would have liked to. Stupid wet lump of coal! I mean, what's the point of an amphibious snorkel-sucking mercenary who hates swimming anyway?" Thomas took a deep swig of his ale.

"Much like a mercenary who uses grappling hooks and is afraid of heights," Charlie muttered under his breath.

"I heard that!" Thomas said.

"Hooks, come on, I'm sure you two can maintain professionalism while in these parts. Speaking of professions, you clearly came looking for an information broker. Well, here I am."

Thomas took another swig of his ale and leaned in closer. "You know my long-term mission, yes?"

"Yes."

"I have a lead."

"Ah, finally! What is it?"

"The man I'm looking for leads an organisation called the Symbicate," Thomas whispered.

"Ah." Charlie's face softened. "You'll have much competition on that front."

"Oh?"

"Yes, most of the hired thugs you see around you today are all after a bounty for such a man as that. There are two high-profile marks in this city at the moment ... well ... three ... well ... technically two are ..." He bit the inside of his cheek. "I have to be careful what I say in public, Hooks. We'll say three, but no one has come close to nabbing Rella in a decade. Anyway, your man, Ringleader, is one of them."

Thomas struggled to follow Charlie's incoherent description of the lay of the land, but the word 'Ringleader' drowned out all the other noise. He gazed around the crowded saloon. The tall, bald guy was now wandering up the stairs to a private room with a girl on each arm while the surrounding tables where he was standing were eyeing each other fiercely.

"Have you given these idiots any viable information?" Thomas turned back to Charlie.

"Not as viable as I'm willing to give you," Charlie said. "I just gave a charming young lady an approximate location, but I can do you a few better. You saved my life once upon a time—I'll even give you mates rates—two colours of the bounty."

"I ain't here for bounty."

"Nevertheless, you are the man with more than cubes driving his quest. My money is on you being the one to kill him," he cleared his throat, "and you being the one to cash in on it afterward."

"Very well, two colours," Thomas agreed.

"See the men at the bar over your right shoulder?" Charlie asked.

Thomas glanced subtly; they were trying to keep their backs to the brewing brawl of tables behind them. He gave Charlie a nod.

"Those two are a part of probably the most reputable smuggling ring in the world—if smugglers could be reputable. They have a long-standing relationship with the Symbicate, probably part of the last vestiges of the Symbicate itself some theorise."

"The Symbicate is dwindling?" Thomas asked.

"They've been bleeding revenue for almost a decade now. Not much honour amongst thieves and assassins. Their ledgers are full of red, and the debt collectors have been coming knocking in a big way—hence the bounties. The ground is falling out from underneath the head of the Symbicate, which is why they have risked returning to this town."

"Risked?" Thomas asked.

"Do you want to know the guy's life story, or do you want to find him?" Charlie snapped. Thomas settled down, and Charlie continued. "Any who … the smuggler's leader—the Symbicate head's business partner—ran a joint operation kidnapping rich people's children and ransoming them off. It was the only thing keeping the organisation afloat. Then some do-gooding hero offed him when they bit off a bit more than they could chew by kidnapping a countess …"

Duchess. Thomas began to grasp the full extent of what he had done weeks previously in the ruins on the island.

"Their last revenue dried up, and now they're fair game, all power lost, it seems. Those men at the bar have been paid handsomely by the man I suspect is the leader of the Symbicate to smuggle him across the sea. Just slightly more than the actual bounty itself, hence their continued loyalty."

"Thank you, Charlie." Thomas rose and headed over to the bar.

"Two colours, Hooks!" Charlie called.

Thomas waved over his shoulder, "Yeah, yeah," and continued along his path.

Charlie went back to his tome. "Ah," he snapped his fingers, "not Frogman! Snipes was the Hired Hero who had checked in." He turned to call after Thomas, but he was out of earshot.

Thomas sauntered between the two table groups, who looked on the verge of breaking out into an all-out brawl. "Gentlemen," he said nonchalantly, and waltzed up to the bar, leaning on it heavily like most of the drunkards around.

"What's the deal *withhhose* guys ya reckon?" he slurred to the two shifty-looking smugglers.

"That tall guy took both their serving girls upstairs and somehow made them blame each other," one smuggler said.

"Now, piss off!" his partner muttered.

"Oh, oh, hey, watch it there, you'll ..." Thomas hiccupped for effect, "hurt my feelings there."

"Look, buddy." The muttering smuggler turned to him, whipping open his coat to show off the large knife he had strapped to one side. "I don't think you heard me."

"Whoa, whoa." Thomas raised his hands defensively, then sheepishly—but obviously—glanced at his own sheathed blades to his side and at his grappling gauntlets on each arm. "I think mine might be bigger than yours."

"Eh, come on, mate." The friendlier smuggler grabbed the menacing one by the shoulder and sat him back down. "Don't make a scene. And you, buddy, better leave."

"Don't make a scene, eh?" Thomas asked, dropping his slur. "In a place like this? One would think you two are trying to hide in plain sight or something." The menacing smuggler stiffened. "Got a big job on tonight?"

The nicer of the smugglers slowly craned his neck to glare at him. *He is obviously the bigger threat out of the pair,* Thomas noted.

"You better move on, friend," he said, politely, calmly, threateningly.

"How's about we all move on to a quieter place?" Thomas said.

The lead smuggler whispered to his friend, "Meet you at the pickup point," and side kicked one of the patrons at the table into their rivals.

The effect was instantaneous—the entire saloon erupted into a full-on brawl. Tables flipped over, bottles and chairs broke over heads, people dove over counters, and all the while, the player piano kept up its jaunty tune.

The lead smuggler vanished in an instant, but Thomas—knocked around by kerfuffling bodies—kept track of the less restrained smuggler as he bolted for a just previously broken window, and dove through it.

"I haven't had a good chase in a while!" Thomas shouted as he wove around sparring patrons, vaulted over the bar woman who was crouching down by a support pillar, and burst through the swinging doors.

Thomas laughed; the brawl had somehow spilled outside too. But he spotted his quarry, dusting broken glass from his coat as he bolted down a side street. Thomas grappled onto one of the crisscrossing street bridges above and gave chase, leaping, vaulting, and grapple swinging between the buildings.

The smuggler, unaware of his pursuer, took a staircase that led up into one of the enclosed bridges. A wooden lattice slat shaded the innards from what Thomas imagined was a harsh sun in the summer. He swung and burst through one of the slats.

He collided with a man who had a knife drawn on a young lady, knocking him out cold.

"Oh, I'm so sorry ..." Thomas started, but hesitated when he recognised the lady. "Oh, hi, Tara."

"Hello ..." she said. She elbowed the thug who had been restraining her from the rear and slipped out of the open hole Thomas had made. "Gotta go, Thomas, sorry!"

"See ya!" Thomas looked down the bridge where the smuggler had stopped in his tracks at the entrance. He considered for a moment and then bolted in the other direction. Thomas turned to the two thugs, one groaning and the other out cold. "I really am very sorry about interrupting you, but I probably just saved you from whatever she was preparing to do." Thomas bowed and bolted down the bridge.

Thomas exited the bridge and grappled up onto a rooftop, startling a Mason long gun pair who were on watch. He gave them little thought and continued after the smuggler as he scurried around the lower streets.

"Hey!" the guards shouted. "Halt!"

But Thomas was already away, striding across shop sign rafters and gutters and leaping out to grapple and swing, trying not to let his gut rise up into his throat each time.

The smuggler eventually reached a T-intersection that ended with a gatehouse. The road was sparsely populated and heavily guarded; he barrelled through the guards and past the gated checkpoint that led into another quadrant of the city.

The guards called after him but gave no chase. Thomas swung down into the perpendicular street from the T-intersection and bolted straight ahead for the checkpoint.

"Halt!" they cried as Thomas sprinted towards them.

"You let him go through!" Thomas cried as he continued.

"He doesn't have a symbioid, halt!" Two long gunners crossed their guns to bar Thomas's path.

"Damn, he's getting away!" Thomas cursed.

"For what reason do you chase this man? Is it for a quest?" a guard asked.

"Yes!" Thomas said.

"That is acceptable ..."

Must be so easy to get away with things in this town, Thomas thought.

"But no symbioid woven can enter the zombie quadrant," the guard finished.

"Why not?"

"They will take control of your symbioid. You'll become one of their puppets!"

"What? That's not true. Why hasn't this information spread around the world?" Thomas countered. "I don't believe it one bit!"

"I'm not responsible for your lack of worldly knowledge, foreigner!" the guard responded. "Now leave this area immediately!"

Thomas was going to argue more, but there was a commotion from the street he swung down from. A group of long gun pairs bustled towards them.

"Ho there!" the guard who had been arguing with Thomas called.

"Ho there! We have reports that this one was chasing an unarmed man."

"It is okay, friend, he is on a quest."

"Oh, well, that is okay then."

"How the hell is that okay, you moon rock morons?" Thomas screamed. "How do you nitwits maintain any law and order in this town?"

"Now, sir," the captain of the newcomers said, "you're being quite rude, and we won't have a bar of it!"

Thomas gritted his teeth.

"Now, so long as you don't impede on anyone who is not involved in your quest, we will allow you free passage. But make no mistake, we will not tolerate law breaking. We have just been rounding up brawlers at a local tavern. There were no quests being fulfilled there."

"How many collars?" the checkpoint guard captain asked.

"About half a dozen so far."

Their exchange filtered from Thomas's mind as he eyed the checkpoint. He'd never get through these guards. But perhaps he could grapple over them. He gazed upwards. The buildings along this side of the street had been walled together, separating the city from whatever dwelled within. And he could feel his quarry gaining distance with every breath. His chance at vengeance slipped through his fingers while he played nice with these incompetents.

He quickly aimed upwards and launched a grapple. His feet were barely dragged from the ground when two of the Mason guards tackled him. Thomas landed with a grunt but continued trying to spool himself upwards when one of the long gunners whacked at the grapple point with his bayonet.

It clattered to the ground and spooled back into his gauntlets.

"Cogrust," Thomas swore.

"I'm afraid, sir, that we will have to arrest you too. It's for your own good."

"Crap, cogrusting, shit!" Thomas beat the ground.

"IT'S RELLA!" someone shouted.

Something landed in the midst of them. The two guards pinning Thomas were flung into the air, and he managed to struggle up to see a creature laying waste to the surrounding men. Tendrils flung from a bundle in his hand, and he moved with a strange, disjointed grace—unreadable, unpredictable, and dangerous.

Rella.

He spun to face Thomas, who started back as Rella strode over to him. He was tall, and like his wanted poster, he was wearing a top hat and monocle with a dapper black tailcoat and red cravat, which made his bushy white moustache even more pronounced. His deep umber skin suggested he was from Masonville, but his flesh was dull.

Thomas raised his gauntlet to launch a grapple at the thing, but Rella raised an arm.

"There will be no need for that, Mister Marrow," he said in a polite, accent-less voice.

"How do you know my name?" Thomas asked.

The group of guards down the street deployed themselves, which stopped Rella from replying. Each man without a long gun formed a rank and took a knee, and then the gunmen behind them lowered their weapons over the nooks in their pauldrons to fire.

"That's a bother," Rella said as he knelt by Thomas and expanded his bundle-like weapon.

"Is that an umbrella?" Thomas asked.

There was an explosion, not a trumpeting sound like a blunderbuss, but a precise cracking like a thunderclap. The umbrella pinged as a volley was unloaded onto it. It expanded more to protect the two men on the ground.

"They're firing even though they'll hit their own men!?" Thomas yelled over the din.

Rella said nothing, sporting a furrowed brow as more shots pinged off of the umbrella. Thomas realised that all the shots were hitting their mark, hitting their makeshift shield.

Those long guns ARE accurate. "What is that umbrella made of?" he asked.

"Oh, silk I believe, and symbioid sinew for now, of course." Rella smiled.

The shots ceased.

"Reload!" the captain ordered.

"Now's as good a time as any. I'm terribly sorry about this," Rella said as he took Thomas by the arm.

"For wha—What the hell!" he cried as dozens of sinewy tendrils spread out from Rella's hands and imbedded into Thomas's arm.

Against his will, his arm raised and launched a grapple over the checkpoint; then they accelerated up and over the makeshift building wall like they had just been fired from a gun themselves. They jettisoned into the air over the zombie quadrant. Thomas's grapple released despite his attempts to stay attached, and they fell.

Thomas screamed.

Just before impact, Rella's umbrella opened and expanded to an enormous size, slowing their descent until they lightly touched down on the ground. Rella released his tendrils from Thomas's arm and let him collapse to his knees as he calmly collapsed his umbrella.

"What in the three perversities was that?" Thomas screamed. He had never cursed from religion before, but being in Boss's old home and facing down this monstrosity, it seemed fitting.

"Please, Mister Marrow, remain calm."

"You took control of my symbioid! Of my very body!"

"Regrettable but necessary, I assure you."

Thomas struggled up onto his feet—ready to fight—but before he drew his blades, he noticed the surrounding onlookers, dozens of glossy-eyed people, staring blankly as if they were dead.

"I think you'll find, Mister Marrow, that you are outnumbered here … not that you would have stood a chance against me, least not with a symbioid woven into your very skeleton."

Thomas lowered his hands, and the dead-eyed people began to shamble away. They lumbered with that same disjointed grace that Rella fought with. "What is going on?" Thomas asked.

"We have a common enemy, Mister Marrow. I took the liberty of capturing your lead for you. If you wouldn't mind, we could have some tea. I'll answer all your questions, and we can interrogate him together."

"The guards …"

"Know better than to step foot in my territory."

Thomas took a deep breath, trying to collect his thoughts.

"All right," he finally said. "Where's this tea?"

CHAPTER 13

Eric Futruble

Eric cautiously creaked open the steel gate that separated the old Futruble estate from the hubbub of the city. He slinked in, clicking the gate shut behind him, which culled the incessant noise from his abode.

The walls were high and were erected close to the three-storey mansion that Eric had grown up in, with bricks that showcased eloquently patterned masonry. He peered up at his home, filling with a sense of nostalgia that was not ruined by the state of disrepair that the building had fallen into. Breathing in the memories for one last second, he then turned his focus to the task at hand.

"Uncle," he whispered.

He strode up the path to the heavy oaken door and drew his blade—it was ajar, and there was blood seeping out from underneath it. Terror overwhelmed him, and he threw caution to the wind—blinking through the open door and swiping wildly at any who might be lying in wait.

He swiped at air.

The entrance hall—an open atrium that rose up all three levels to the chandeliered ceiling—was littered with bodies.

"Uncle," he whispered again.

None of the bodies belonged to his dear uncle, and only some wore the garb of those who would serve under him; the rest were of various mercenary groups. Eric crouched down and pressed his fingertip into one of the pools of blood.

"Lukewarm." He wiped the blood on the clothes of the deceased before him.

There was a crash from the upper floors and a shout, the trumpeting of a blunderbuss and the clang of metal.

"Uncle!" he roared.

He blinked up the lavish entrance hall stairs to the second floor, finding more bodies and a red-coated mercenary desperately reloading his blunderbuss. He was ramming the shot down the barrel with a steel rod when he noticed Eric, and his eyes went wide.

"Boys! We've got more company!" He raised the blunderbuss, rod still embedded within it—and fired.

Eric had blinked to the upper level before he had pulled the trigger. He heard from safety the resulting explosion as the rod fragmented into a thousand pieces and killed the twitchy moron. On the third-level balcony, Eric saw the last remnants of a desperate melee between two small groups of mercenaries. A servant of the house lay dead at the foot of the study's doors. It was currently being rammed by two members of a gang who had the numbers advantage over their competitors. Without a moment's hesitation, Eric blinked into the fray, catching the brawling parties off guard and swiping through their confused melee within seconds. The two mercenaries ramming the door, who were coated in drab greys like some of the others who had been fighting, turned to face him.

"You killed our boys!" one said. He was older and sported a bushy grey beard.

"You'll pay for that, you pompous swine!" the other said, an elderly woman.

"You're 'The Family of Mercs'?" Eric asked, readying his blade to fight the two.

"We were, until you killed our sons and daughters!" the woman cried.

"Most of them were already dead. Now you are trespassers in my house. Depart, or I shall depart you."

The parent mercenaries screamed and charged forth. Eric—breathing erratically from his blinking exertions—braced for the ferocious struggle. The doors behind them swung open, and a wounded servant carrying two pistols shot them in the back in quick succession—bam, bam—then slumped onto the ground.

The parents fell to the ground with choked grunts. Eric rushed past their bodies to hold the servant in his arms.

"James? James, stay with me," Eric said.

He put pressure on the servant's wounded side.

"Master Eric?"

"Yes, James, what happened here?"

"Oh, Master Eric! Constantine said you would come! We've been dodging all sorts of undesirables for weeks now.

These two groups attacked us simultaneously. If it were not for them competing for Master Constantine's head, I would not have managed to help him slip away."

Eric's heart sank as James's eyes grew vacant. "Where is he, faithful servant?"

"A s-safe house by the Buttress Quarter. It is close to his escape route from the city, which he will take tonight. It will have this symbol at its door." James made a show to reach for his coat pocket.

Eric helped him retrieve the small amulet; it looked like a strange coin with an orb-like symbol embossed into its centre and an "S" much like the one embossed on the letter Constantine had sent him.

"Find him, Eric, save him." James breathed his last breath.

"I will, old friend, I will."

#

After mourning the death of his uncle's servants, Eric left the bitter estate. All of his childhood nostalgia had seeped away like the blood under the doorframe. He could offer no ceremony for his allies, as more mercenaries could show up at any moment.

He wandered slowly in a haze throughout the bustling streets, heading ever onward towards the Buttress Quarter. He remembered it vividly from his youth. It was an area that an old Master Mason had purchased centuries ago in order to hone his cathedral-making craft before travelling around the world to build grand places of worship for all faiths. Back then, it was a quarter of the size of Masonville.

Now the city had grown enough that it engulfed the sacred space.

It was made of rows upon rows of tunnels and bridges and canals and spires, all latticed with increasingly intricate buttresses which the Master Mason had repeated again and again in order to hone his craft. It hosted spires and intertwining levels and deep underground sections, which mazed together to form the perfect escape route towards the nearby docks. Which is why—Eric was sure—Constantine had chosen it.

Eric's ears prickled, and he spun on the spot.

A busy street, merchants haggling with passing patrons, a passing guard troop, normal enough. But something was off. Eric dismissed it as the over workings of his grieving mind and turned back to his path. However, the eerie feeling of being followed persisted.

The sun was dipping below the city walls, casting orange hues across the white stones of the surrounding buildings, shining the streets in heavenly beams when Eric found the safe house. The Buttress Quarter loomed down the street, an entangled web of madness, art, and stone, and the tiny house—squeezed in between rows of similar estates—sat unassumingly in the afternoon light.

Eric marched up to the door. It was marked above by the same golden emblem on the coin that he had been given by his dying servant. He knocked. A peep hatch opened at face level, and a wide blunderbuss poked out, nudging Eric's face.

"Who goes there?" the gravelly voice said from behind the door.

"An ally to an old man," Eric replied.

There was a click—not the lock of the door, but the hammer of the blunderbuss.

"An old man has no more allies." The voice was chilling.

"What about nephews?"

There was a pause, and then the gun withdrew from Eric's face, leaving a shadowed recess in the peep hatch.

"Eric?"

"Uncle!"

"Eric!" The door swung open, and a wrinkled, yet powerful hand shot out, grabbing Eric by the collar and pulling him into darkness.

Eric stumbled into the small hallway and turned to find Constantine in the dimness, locking the door again before placing a large beam across the threshold.

He turned to his nephew. "You got my message then?"

"I did, Uncle, what is happening?"

"Oh, my boy!" Constantine cried, rushing in and hugging the younger viscount. "I can't tell you how good it is to see a friendly face. But I fear I have dragged you into more danger."

"What is happening, Uncle?" Eric asked again, returning the embrace.

"I have made a right mess of things, my boy, and now my circle of enemies is closing in." He pulled away and regarded the expectant Eric with squinting silver eyes. "Come along, I have a pot of tea on. I'll tell you everything."

Minutes later Eric was sitting in a cramped lounge room in the dark and shuttered safe house, which had worn stone walls coloured by age and an eclectic mix of red drapery over the furniture. Constantine poured him a cup of tea from a pot in a bright woolly cosy. The steaming dark liquid brought warmth to the viscount's cold, fatigued hands.

Constantine sat with his own cup and sighed. "I take it you went to the old estate? I suppose James and the boys did not fare well against those two brutish groups."

"James died in my arms." Eric sipped from his tea. Constantine was silent. "Why did James die in my arms? Why is this city teeming with bounty hunters, half of which seem to be after you specifically?"

"More than half," Constantine corrected. "You know the manner of my secret work, boy. You understand that in my works for the greater good that I must take measures to protect myself and my family."

"I understand as much as I can without knowing what the work actually is, Uncle," Eric said flatly. "Perhaps it is time I knew?"

Constantine stirred his tea with his finger, considering his words carefully. "I have a secret identity—a call sign—if you will, 'Ringleader.'"

"Ringleader?"

"I am the informal head of a formal—or what used to be formal—organisation. Underground, operating independently of any monarch or government." Constantine continued. "We called ourselves the Symbicate."

"I have heard whispers of such an organisation," Eric said, "but I figured it was the bogeymen tales of criminals."

"In a sense, we were. We employed and contested with such various criminal groups. We developed a bit of a reputation."

Eric furrowed his brow. "You *were* criminals?"

"In a manner of speaking, in the name of the greater good, of course," Constantine answered.

"And what was the greater good?"

"Our mission was to reunite the symbioids together, into their true entity." Constantine paused. When Eric showed no signs of interjecting with questions, he nodded to himself and continued. "Patient as ever, Eric, I am proud. We found certain conscious symbioids which provided us with information when more than one or two were woven into a host. The shattered moon, as you know, was once whole, and it was occupied by a single entity ... We think it called itself a guardian, but we referred to it as the Symbioid. It watched over us from the cosmos until a cataclysm tore it asunder, and the scattered body of the being fell to our soil amongst the debris."

"This is a bit much," Eric said, massaging his arm, thinking of blink woven into his body. "I've heard the theories, of course, but if what you are saying is actually true, it must have been akin to a god."

Constantine's eyes grew distant. "Oh yes, my boy, imagine."

"So what happened?"

"Failure. We tracked down as many 'living' symbioids as we could and combined them, hoping to find some remnant of the conjoined consciousness, to protect our world from future cataclysms ... the danger still lingers out in the black deep."

"And?"

"What we gathered must have created a fragmented mind of the Symbioid. And in its confused state, it attacked, resulting in the zombie quadrant. It destroyed our workshops and took over scores of host citizens."

"And it stopped once it gained enough wherewithal to know it wasn't being attacked?" Eric surmised.

Constantine didn't answer at first, but eventually took a breath to speak. "Maybe, sure ... but we could keep it at bay long enough with a device we used to harvest symbioids; it has a symbioid itself in it with that specific ability. Sadly, the people of Masonville did not see the merit of our endeavour. They stripped us of our slaves ..." Eric shot a look to his uncle, "and ousted us from the city. We had many debtors whom we thought we could pay after our success, so we subsisted on ever-diminishing operations. Until finally, our last stream of cubes dried up when authorities shut down our last proper operation just weeks ago. Now the net is closing."

"Slaves?" Eric said. "We actually had slaves?"

"Oh yes, Masonville outlawed them only a few years ago. We had many. Your nanny was one."

"My nanny was a slave?" Eric stood and threw his tea against the wall. "I thought she loved me. She always did what I asked! But she was just following orders! How dare you claim to fight for the greater good and possess slaves?"

Constantine was unperturbed by Eric's outburst. "And our servants are no different?"

"They choose to work for us! We pay them, and they can come and go as they please!"

"Look, Eric, there is much about me you still don't understand."

"So I'm finding out. I'm finding it very difficult to understand you right now ... Uncle."

Constantine sipped the last of his tea and groaned as he rose. "Nephew, we can argue ethics once we are safe. Time has come for us to make for our last refuge across the sea. Now you can help me, or watch the same man who has loved you like a son die ... on principle."

Eric gritted his teeth. "Let us leave then, but don't assume I can ever forgive you for keeping this from me."

Constantine chuckled.

"You laugh at my outrage?"

"I thought you knew she was a slave this whole time." He continued to chuckle. "Pretty much any of the Baul Islanders on this continent were slaves or descendants of slaves. For a smart man, nephew, you are quite naive."

"Don't mock me. You don't know what trials I overcame to reach you here. Now let's go."

"Let me grab my coat," Constantine said.

Eric was waiting by the door when Constantine returned, wearing an elegant golden frock cloak.

"Cogrust! What is that?" Eric said, horror and dread dawning on him, recalling Thomas's tale of the men who killed his father and stole his blinking symbioid. The symbioid that Eric now possessed and was beginning to think was not passed down from his own father.

"It marks me as a high-ranking member of the Symbicate," Constantine said matter-of-factly.

"My blinking symbioid was not from my father, was it?" Eric asked. "It came from a man called Marrow."

Constantine started. "How do you know that name?"

"You said you tracked down symbioids. How did you extract them from the people who had already woven to them?"

"Come now, Eric."

"How?"

Constantine looked on sombrely. "We removed the hosts, bribed with cubes, coerced with violence—any way necessary for the greater good."

"And sold their children into slavery after the fact?" Eric spat.

"How do you know that?" Constantine spat back. "You know what? Forget about it! We are running late, and you should trust me in the knowledge that it was for the greater good!"

"And how many great people died for your good?"

Constantine chuckled. "Wordplay won't sway me."

Eric grinded his teeth again. "So you have half the bounty hunters in this town after you because you're the ringleader of a criminal organisation ... *the* criminal organisation ... and the other half?"

"The other half are after me, the real me, Constantine Futruble, because once I lost the funds to pay off the authorities, they put a warrant out for my arrest ... Two of the biggest bounties of a lifetime, one for each of my alter egos."

Eric growled, "And there is one among them who is after you purely for revenge ... come on, let's go." He barged out the door.

The sun was setting, and the air was crisp and cool. A dark figure waited across the empty street.

"So why did you tell me the blink came from my father?" Eric asked, as his uncle exited the door and shut it behind him, locking it with a key from a jingling chain.

"Your father was friends with Barty Marrow. He was stricken with his friend's death so much that he—well, he fell on the drink hard, died in an alley somewhere. The blink somehow managed to stay with us in the confusion after the zombie quadrant … I thought your father would have wanted you to have it."

He turned as he was pocketing the key, and the shadowy figure from across the street walked over.

"No," Constantine went white, "Decibel?"

"Decibel?" Eric asked.

"Decibel!" the shadowy cloaked man shouted, louder than any living man should be able to.

The surrounding air began to shimmer. Constantine began to claw back inside his safe house but fumbled with the keys, and they clattered to the ground uselessly.

"Eric, we must stop him!" Constantine blubbered. "Quickly!"

Eric blinked forward while drawing his blade to rush and strike the man down. The next thing he knew, he was on the ground, writhing in pain and clutching at his ears. The shadowy figure strode over to Eric with an echoing laugh; the air around him shimmered and wobbled as a high-pitched sound drove itself into Eric's brain. He was sure that he was screaming, but he could hear nothing but the sinister laugh and the stabbing sound piercing his ears.

"Nice try, blinker," he could somehow hear the man say. "But my symbioid is vibrating the air too much for your tendrils to cope."

Eric roared—or at least he thought he did. He pushed the pain in his mind aside and rose to slash and swipe at his attacker. His vision throbbed, his mind swam, and each effort was like trying to force motion through water. The man simply stepped around his attacks, calmly drawing his own blade.

After a few desperate attacks, Eric broke off and squared back up against Decibel. He brought his blade in close, minimising the distance he would need to block any incoming blows in his slow state.

The man sniffed a laugh, and charged in. The moment before he struck, the shimmering and piercing noise intensified, and Eric was floored backward—his vision went white with the pain of the sound in his head. His blade scattered what may as well have been half the world away. Decibel stood over him, with his sword raised for the finishing blow.

Constantine charged in from the side wielding a golden orb and tackled the distracted Decibel down into the ground. He pressed the orb against Decibel's chest and clicked a button; the orb opened and a strange white light shone from it as Decibel writhed in pain. Sinews were torn from Decibel and siphoned into the little golden device. The warbling air and high-pitched sound died along with the siphoned sinews, and the pain inside of Eric's head subsided.

The orb clicked shut, and Eric could hear his heart in his head, the breeze throughout the streets, the screaming of children in the surrounding houses, and the terrified moaning of Decibel.

"What have you done?" he screamed.

"I have silenced you, traitor!" Constantine rammed a knife into Decibel's heart, ending his pained moans with one last crescendo.

Constantine rolled off the corpse, and for a while the two viscounts lay there panting.

"What is a Decibel?" Eric managed to ask after a minute.

"Decibel was one of my finest agents. His symbioid allowed him to manipulate sound, probably caused too much vibration for your symbioid to split and blink your body across any useful distance."

"He was your agent?" Eric asked, struggling up again, aware of the people who were coming outside to investigate the disturbance.

"As soon as we couldn't pay him, he turned on us. He must have been watching our estate when you turned up and then followed you here." Constantine also struggled to rise. "Come now, nephew, that commotion will bring guards and any bounty hunter within miles of us. Come on!"

The two men took each other in their arms and stumbled off to the nearby Buttress Quarter. By the time they entered the labyrinth of tunnels, they could hear the commotion of the growing scene behind them. But at least they were safe.

"Can you stand on your own?" Eric asked, releasing his uncle once they had run through several tunnels and over canals and under spires and bridges.

"I think so. I should be fine. That was a close one," Constantine said.

"All right," Eric said, releasing him, "I will take point. Stay close to me."

"Aye, Eric, good lad."

The two walked on in silence, making their way through the labyrinth. It was dark as the sun set. The shattered moon painted itself against the deep black star-studded sky. It was the only light when the sky was exposed, pale green and casting foreboding shadows throughout the structures. Whenever they were hidden from the sky, there were rows of old-fashioned gas lamps, burning dim but constantly. Eric found their warm glow more a comfort than the moon's—it meant they were concealed from outward sight.

After half an hour, they came to a quadrangle, open to the sky and surrounded with intricate buttresses and spires. Eric cautiously stepped out into the open to reach the other side of the expanse when a sound stopped him.

His ears tweaked in recognition. It was the sound of a grapple being fired.

"Viscount!" a voice boomed, as a figure in the gloom swooped down from a spire and landed in the shadows.

Constantine stepped up behind Eric. "I recognise that face," he whimpered.

"Oh, no." Eric paled as the furious Thomas Marrow emerged from the shadows.

The two friends faced off against one another.

CHAPTER 14

Tara Night

Tara stalked her target from the rooftops. She did not slink and hide like she ordinarily would when tracking from a vantage point. The rooftops of this town were accessible to the public, and the sun was out—shining brightly through the chilled air.

She moved through throngs of pedestrians as they shuffled from landing to skywalk to staircase and so on; such was the crisscrossing nature of the city's infrastructure. Tracing through the crowds while stalking a target was simple for one such as her; however, she was disconcerted by tracking someone below her while also navigating people above.

These two kinds of stalking just don't mix, she mused to herself as her target grabbed a trinket from a stall below and bolted from the shouting merchant.

She took off after him, knocking over several slow goers on her path. Her target was a young street urchin whom she knew would know the lay of the land. He was being pursued by some ruffian under the employ of the markets. He would soon gain on the child and beat him senseless, unless she intervened.

She leaped from a staircase, landing onto the balcony of a lower level as the child turned down a narrow alley, the ruffian hot on his heels. Tara landed on a balcony cafe where two patrons were enjoying a steaming cup of something and knocked their table over. Oblivious to the patrons' shouts, she bounded up and vaulted the balcony railing and onto the street—dashing into the alley.

It was a dead end; the street urchin was being pulled from the far wall by the ruffian as Tara sprinted forward. The ruffian slammed the child against the ground and planted a vicious kick into his gut. Tara leaped into the air as the child gasped in pain and smashed her knee into the back of the ruffian's head.

He slammed forward into the wall and collapsed, knocked out cold. Tara stumbled back, panting, and leaned forward with her hands on her knees as the child groaned and stood.

"A kid, like you," she said between gasps as she struggled to control her breathing, "should know, not to, run into a dead end."

The kid coughed and spat out a small amount of blood. "A kid like me would know the lady stalking him for the past half an hour might intervene if she hadn't taken him already." He smirked through the pain.

"You knew I was there?" Tara asked, rising to her full height as she regained control of her breathing.

"Lady," the kid responded, "every other kid I encountered pointed you out to me."

"Cogrust," Tara swore.

The piercing voice of the Night Mother echoed throughout her mind. *STUPID GIRL!*

"So," the kid said tentatively, "if you don't want to hurt me, why are you following me?"

Tara slid a green cube out from her coat pocket. "I'm after information."

The child's eyes went wide with wonder as she tossed it to him. "And you're paying me upfront?" The kid gasped in disbelief.

"No. Half now, half after you help me find my target."

The kid pocketed the cube swiftly before reality decided to take it from him. "How may I serve you, lady?"

"Is anyone trying to skip town since all of these bounty hunters started showing up?"

The kid thought for a moment. "Yeah, actually."

#

"Are you sure?" Tara asked, eyeing the seedy, bulging tavern.

"As sure as ever, lady. The men you want are smugglers, like to hang out at the end of the bar before a job. And they *do* have a job tonight, sneaking someone out of town."

"Two of them?" Tara asked again.

"Two here, yeah."

"And you're sure?"

"Sally, the girl over yonder." He gestured to another street urchin eyeing them from across the way. "Saw them slip in just half an hour ago. Now be careful in there, lady, some of the types that frequent this place would slit your throat just for looking at them wrong."

Tara squinted at the little boy, making a show of sizing him up, then with a half smirk tossed him another green cube. "All right, kid, get clear of here."

The child barely snatched the cube from the air before he bolted and was gone from sight. Tara marvelled at his speed.

"I wonder if I was as cunning as that when I was on the streets," she wondered to herself.

She turned to the tavern. The sign above read 'The Jaunt Saloon' and it reeked of anything but class. Though she did enjoy the roaring piano tune that rang out constantly. She slipped inside without incident.

The inside was even seedier than the outside. It smelled of sweat, alcohol, and worse, that raunchy smell you can't place. But she sighted her targets. There was one problem—there were four smuggler types at the bar, not two.

Damn it! she screamed internally. *Which two are the smugglers?*

She moved around the edge of the tavern, keeping an eye on the four men while looking for her own seat to view the area without arousing suspicion. She came to a conclusion based on how they were interacting. There wasn't a group of four smugglers but two pairs of men sitting side by side in the crammed bar. She had to figure out who were the ones she wanted.

She picked a seat at a bench by a window and waited.

For a while, there was no incident, a minor brawl here, an idle threat there—but there did seem to be trouble brewing.

She could feel it even though she did not know what form it would take. Between her and the bar were three tables: two tables had groups of men playing a game of settlement for cubes, and at another, a lone man sat. He was pale, tall, bald, and wore a black leather military cloak. Tara's mind flickered with recognition, recalling the lessons she had learned of other people in the trade.

Luke Sill ... Cogrust! She raged internally again. *The bloody hit man with a luck symbioid, just MY gear-jammed luck!* She realised she was breathing raggedly and calmed herself. *Remember your training. Skill beats luck. Remember your goal, kill the leader of the Symbicate. Remember the consequences should you fail—death, and your street urchins back home go undefended.*

She took several deep breaths and watched the happenings for a time. Before long, a barwoman showing far too much cleavage waltzed up to her.

"Anything I can get you, hon?" she asked.

"Do you think I could get you some more clothes?" Tara said. "You must be freezing!"

The barwoman smiled warmly. "Well, aren't you just too cute!" She pinched Tara's cheek, causing her to blush.

"Uhhh," Tara started.

"I'll get you something small, hon, on the house," and without a word, the barwoman waltzed off.

Before Tara could make sense of the interaction, she noticed someone new in the bar, speaking with Luke Sill at his table. She was a gorgeous woman in a big green fur coat and a form-fitting blue dress beneath. She also had a ginormous sword strapped to her back. She had dark brown skin—unlike the burnt umber of Mason folk. Tara figured she must be from the Baul Islands, since she kept pulling the thick green coat around her while shivering. But it somehow kept slipping from her shoulders, much to her visible annoyance and Luke's delight.

That luck symbioid is letting him catch a glimpse of her in that dress ... bastard, Tara thought. She leaned in to hear their conversation.

"Fancy seeing you here, Miss Brune," Luke said.

"You as well, Luke," she said, tugging at her coat. "Bloody thing won't stay on! It was sized for a brute."

"Perhaps it would be better if you took it off?" Luke asked, innocently enough.

The one called Brune went to remove it but then stopped, regarding his leering expression. "I'd rather not actually."

He cocked his head. "Interesting. Maybe something better for me is on the horizon?"

"I beg your pardon?" she asked.

"Well, I figured—knowing my luck," he grinned wickedly, "I would bed you upstairs, and you would give me the secret password needed to speak with the broker afterward ... I mean, you just spoke to him for one of your own quests, I'm sure. Usually when I don't get what I want it is because something better is on the horizon."

Brune stood up abruptly. "Typical. Why did I think you were so charming in Shanty Towers?"

"'Cause I'm lucky!" He laughed.

Brune swore and stormed out of the bar, colliding with someone outside.

Tara realised she was clenching her fists. *With all of the good you could use a good luck symbioid for, and he uses it to get laid and use people who trust him? Why I oughta!* She rose to confront the tall hit man but stopped when he stood abruptly.

The barwoman carrying Tara's drink was knocked over by Luke's chair, and she stumbled straight into one of the gambling tables, spilling beer over everyone.

The men cried in outrage and rose with menacing looks towards the barwoman, and she shifted back in fright, crashed into a barwoman serving the other gambling table who also spilled her drinks all over them.

Both tables rose and were making threats against the two women. At this, Luke Sill stepped between the lot and yelled to each table. "It was not the lovely ladies' fault but your own. This table pushed the first barwoman into you guys, and you pushed her back into the other!"

"They what?" the two tables said in unison.

"Why don't I take these girls out of harm's way, and you guys can settle your differences?" Luke escorted the barwomen away from the altercation, taking them between tables of patrons who were eyeing the scene of the brewing brawl, and past the bar, where the bartender was calmly stowing the fine liquor away—standard operating procedure should a tussle break out. The barwomen on each of Luke's arms seemed to be grateful for his intervention and directed him towards the rickety stairs by the bar that led up into the saloon's rooms. "And maybe you two could help me out afterwards?" Tara heard him ask as he left earshot.

She shot a glance back to the tables. Each table was staring the other down menacingly. And out of the four men at the bar, two were getting agitated.

They must be the smugglers to be so antsy, she thought.

As Luke waltzed away, the two antsy ones got up and made for the door. Tara followed them out of the saloon.

The two men quickly dashed down an alley street and up a flight of stairs on the side of a building, heading towards an enclosed bridge between two rooftops. Tara sped up the stairs and around the corner of the enclosed bridge to be greeted by the two men she had been following, only they had knives drawn.

Before she could react, one had the blade pressed against her neck, and the other rushed behind to hold her.

"Why are you following us?" one said.

"I just want information on your smuggling operation," she said calmly. "I'm after the man you're smuggling out tonight."

The man before her took a step back. "We ain't smugglers! We're wanted thieves, wanted to get out of that tavern before a brawl erupted and the guards turned up."

"Oh ..." Tara said, realising that the smugglers would be the two men still at the bar. "Cogrust. Well, gentlemen, excuse my intrusion then. I'll just head back."

"We ain't letting you go back!" the one in front said.

"I was afraid you'd say that," Tara replied. She readied herself to break free and fight.

But something stopped her. A man sprinted into the enclosed bridge on the far side, saw the encounter, and hesitated.

Tara and the two thugs glanced in his direction.

Then her ears tweaked to the familiar sound of a grappling hook. The shade slat on the side of the enclosed bridge erupted in splinters, and the man before Tara was knocked out cold beneath the weight of Thomas Marrow as he swung through.

Tara and the man restraining her blinked.

"Oh, I'm so sorry …" Thomas started before recognising Tara. "Oh, hi, Tara."

"Hello …" she said. She elbowed the thug who had been restraining her from the rear and slipped out of the open hole Thomas had made. "Gotta go, Thomas, sorry!"

"See ya!" he called to her as she hit the street below with a roll and bolted back for the Jaunt Saloon.

"Stupid girl, stupid girl, STUPID GIRL!" she said with each stride.

She rounded a corner and found that the saloon had erupted into chaos, brawling had broken out onto the streets, and guards were rushing in from each direction to keep it under wraps.

Tara backed into a side street to avoid the guards' attention and skulked away. The side street was empty save for one cloaked figure sitting against a wall.

"Stupid girl, what are you going to do now?" she said to herself, as she smacked her head with her palms. "Stupid, stupid girl!"

"Well, you got that right," the cloaked figure on the street said as Tara passed.

Tara spun on the spot, drawing her blade on the neck of the apparent beggar. A beggar in a fine black cloak. A chill ran down Tara's spine.

The figure looked up from beneath the hood, showing a young woman's pale olive face within the shadowy recess, a face obscured by a pair of blue-tinted, brass-encased goggles.

"Billie?" Tara said, stepping back and lowering her blade.

"In the flesh." She rose with a smile. "And my, have you jammed things up!"

"Are you here to kill me then?" Tara asked. "'Cause stupid or not, I won't go down without a fight!"

"No, you haven't failed your mission yet. Actually, I'm here to fail mine. I'm here to help you."

"You, help *me*?" Tara asked.

"I'm not as cruel as the Night Mother would have you believe, Tara. I was pressed into her service at a young age, like you … Only, I embraced the darkness to survive. You seem defiant in maintaining some innocence, and for that, I respect you. I want you to succeed."

"How can I succeed, Billie? My lead escaped!"

"Did he now?" Without a word, Billie walked down the street and turned a corner into a dark alleyway.

Tara checked to make sure no one was watching—the guards were still preoccupied with the brawl around the corner—and followed.

She turned into the alley and found Billie standing beside one of the smugglers. He was dead.

Tara gasped, and tried to cover up the sound by drawing it out into a sigh. "He isn't much use to me dead, Billie!"

"I broke him quite quickly, sweet Tara—don't shudder—it saved you the trouble."

"So you know where the head of the Symbicate will be?" Tara asked, suppressing the feeling of her skin crawling at the sight of the mutilated corpse.

"I have known for a while." Billie cocked her head.

"Then why kill this man?"

"To make it seem like you did your job should any other Night assassins turn up!" she said harshly.

Tara stumbled back, conditioned in her training under Billie to react fearfully.

"Now, Tara, let me take you to your quarry."

#

"How can you see down here?" Tara asked.

"Quiet!" Billie hushed. "You're still far too loud, Tara. My goggles have a symbioid at work, woven into the lenses. I can see in the dark."

"Convenient," Tara said.

"I know, right?" Billie chuckled quietly.

They had been winding through sewers for hours, and had come to a grating on the side of a large, open quadrangle within an area known as the Buttress Quarter.

"And now we wait," Billie said.

They didn't have to wait long. The footsteps of two men entered the echoing space. One tentatively stepped out into the open—a bodyguard—Tara assumed. She caught a flicker of a golden-trimmed green coat in the ghastly light of the moon.

No, she thought in horror. *Eric?*

Then a sound rang out that turned her blood to ice, the sound of a grapple being fired.

Thomas?

The stories that the two had shared on their journey to Masonville materialised and wove together before her mind. Eric's uncle needed protecting because so many people were after him, and the man Thomas was hunting for revenge was Eric's uncle ... it all made so much senseless sense.

"Viscount!" Thomas's voice boomed as he swooped down from a spire and landed in the shadows.

The garish, pale green moonlight accented the viscous-looking lines of fury etched into Thomas's face. True fury, fury that Tara had not witnessed in him before. His footsteps as he emerged from the shadows echoed across the hard surfaces in the labyrinthine space of harsh angles and twists and turns. Eric's eyes went wide, the realisation of the coming conflict settling into his posture.

The other man with Eric stepped forward. "I recognise that face," he whimpered.

"Oh, no." Eric paled as the furious Thomas Marrow emerged from the shadows.

"Get ready to make your move, Tara," Billie commanded, oblivious to her distress.

Tara lamented, readying herself as the two friends faced off against each other.

CHAPTER 15

Thomas Marrow

Thomas eyed the steaming black liquid of the chipped mug. He glanced back up at the creature who had offered it to him. A stiff-backed Mason man with lifeless eyes, dull skin, and strange, disjointed movements. He was distracted by the loud slurping of Rella sitting across the table from him. Looking over, Rella was wiping away droplets of tea from his bushy moustache.

"That is a lovely cup of tea, thank you," Rella said.

The thing that had served them said nothing, simply turning and shuffling away to stoke the fire in the ruined apartment they occupied. The rooftop had partially collapsed, leaving scattered debris and the sight of the clear blue sky as it faded with the afternoon.

"How do you find your tea, Thomas?" Rella asked.

Thomas glanced down at the tea again, then back at the zombie who had served them, then back to Rella.

"Is it safe?" he asked.

Rella stifled a chuckle. "Perhaps not," he replied. "Mason tea is a bit stronger than what you would be used to."

Thomas stiffened at this. "I like my tea strong … I'm not a savage." He sipped tentatively at the steaming fluid, having risen to Rella's goading.

Rella chuckled again and sipped some more. After dabbing away the moisture from his moustache, he removed his hat—revealing a bald head—and placed it on the table. Then he let his monocle fall from his eye and tucked it away in his waistcoat.

Finally getting a clear look at the man's face, Thomas was surprised. His eyes were lifeless like those of the other husks here in the zombie quadrant, but his face and movements were super-animated—if still disjointed. Thomas hazarded another sip from the tea before speaking. "You said you had answers for me?"

"Hmm? Oh, of course. Forgive me, I was caught up in the thrill of a nice hot cuppa." Thomas raised an eyebrow at this. Just an hour ago, they had jettisoned into the air and parachuted down into the middle of this zombie-infested area with the help of an expanding umbrella, and now they were enjoying a hot beverage as if on a lazy afternoon. "Please, ask away." Rella placed his teacup down, leaning in enthusiastically.

"Most pressing matter first: where is the smuggler I was chasing?" Thomas asked.

"Some of my scions are questioning him as we speak—don't worry, we are not hurting him. I am simply putting the fear of the three perversities into him, threatening to turn him into another husk in my legion of the undead." Rella waved his hands in a mock-spooky fashion. "The things these morons believe." He cradled his teacup, shaking his head before taking another large slurp.

"I thought you said we would interrogate him together?" Thomas asked.

"I figured that this way is more speedy. That way we can gain the information we need, and you can get a handle on the current situation," Rella replied.

"All right, I'll bite," Thomas said. "If I shouldn't believe that you are the head of legions of the undead ... what should I believe? Who are you? What are you?"

Rella considered him for a moment before answering. "I am the enemy of your enemy, of the man called Ringleader, who controls what is left of the Symbicate—the man who murdered your father and sold your sister into slavery to die."

Thomas's mug cracked under his grip, and the hot liquid spilled down his hand and onto his pants. He took no notice of the pain. "How do you know so much?" he asked.

"Because when the circumstances that allowed me to exist were created—the Blink that had woven with your father imparted some knowledge onto my awareness. I recognise your face, Thomas, and I feel a sense of belonging to your family, based on the tender kinship your father and Blink shared."

Thomas stifled a sob. "So symbioids are sentient."

Rella bobbed his head from side to side. "To a degree."

"Are you a symbioid?"

"To a degree. Honestly, I'm not entirely sure what I am ..." Rella looked away.

"Then start from the beginning, start from the circumstances that led to your existence," Thomas instructed.

Rella smiled. His teeth were worn and thin. "Methodical, truly the son of a tinkerer." He stared down into his tea, and the steam curled around in wisps as the wind blew gently through the ruined building. He seemed to be considering how to tell his story, then finally sighed. "I'll start with some context. As you've probably heard theorised, the symbioids that inhabit your world were once woven into the very moon itself, as a single, unimaginably powerful entity. But then we … I? What I was once a part of was attacked."

"The moon was attacked?" Thomas leaned back in his chair and gazed into the sky through the broken roof.

"Yes … no … I was … something on the moon was attacked. From what I can manage to piece together from my fragmented memory, we were hit by a single, incomprehensibly dense object. One launched at us from some enemy across the cosmos. Much of me … of us … died or was injured." He stroked the rim of his cup in a soothing manner, trying to keep his composure. "As the moon shattered under the impact and bombarded the planet with meteorites, so did the symbioids. Pieces of the body which allowed it to function with mechanical movement, your 'dead' symbioids, and pieces which held onto some measure of their former intelligence, possessing abilities that helped my former self thrive and communicate on the moon."

"Communicate with what?" Thomas asked.

"Other life-forms like me … From what I can gather, we were but a single cog in a celestial machine, until something broke. I believe their purpose was to protect their host planets, from what … I do not know. Perhaps the thing that destroyed us."

"Their purpose?"

"Our," Rella corrected. "It is confusing being split for centuries," he hastily added.

"What in all of the universe could cause so much destruction?"

"You are carrying a part of it, I am sure." Rella smiled.

"What?"

"Why the thing everyone on this stupid world uses for currency nowadays, your cubes!"

"What?!" Thomas pulled out his cube from his pocket. It fit into the palm of his hand and was a pale green, hinting at sliding into blue territory as he had spent much on his journey. "But this is harmless."

"As it is, yes. But I believe it is the product of someone who can manipulate the light wave-particle nature of things."

"The what?" Thomas asked. "Sounds like wizardry."

Rella sighed. "Do not trouble yourself with the science, friend. All you need to know is that when enough of these cubes slide together, it starts to generate immense mass, slipping from weightlessness to … weight-fullness. One by itself weighs as if it is practically a beam of light, but have billions of them, maybe even trillions, fit them together to create a cube that grows blacker than the void and launch it at impossible speeds … Well, you've seen what the moon looks like today."

Thomas regarded his cube with wonder. "And why do we place such value on them?"

Rella shrugged. "You lot are simple. When the Guardian fell to the earth, so did many of these cubes when they scattered upon impact. I guess your ancestors thought they were valuable and hoarded them … that perceived value seems to have stuck. It's as useful a currency as ever, I suppose—can't be forged, easily transported, so why not?"

Thomas pocketed his cube again. "All right, so where do you come in?"

"There was an organisation that gleaned insight into the true nature of symbioids and sought to reunite them in order to 'protect' the world from future threats," Rella answered.

"That doesn't seem so bad?" Thomas said in a questioning tone.

"Well, their measure of protection is control, which in reality was thinly veiled self-satisfaction. They would have been the most powerful people in the world if they succeeded. They called themselves the Symbicate. They tracked down as many symbioids as they could, killing those who would not give theirs up willingly … hence your father's death. And ten years ago, they had enough to warrant an experiment. I emerged. I was angry—I lashed out … at them, at everyone. Sinews of mine infected all of the 'zombies' you see today.

"This body you see before you today, I believe he was a high-ranking politician, had a symbioid which increased his intellectual capacities, which is why I can use him to interact with the world so fluently." He smiled. "From the fragments of his remaining mind, I think he was a good man—used his intelligence to come to the conclusion that altruism was the best path forward for prosperity. Set in motion the outlawing of slavery just before the end, not that it mattered.

"The Symbicate believed outright power was the way forward, and now they must be stopped. And thanks to your actions with the young duchess, you dropped the floor from under them. Since their failure, they have been hanging on by a thread, and now the net is closing, and they even ventured to return to this city, their only safe refuge, which allowed me to pick a few more off … Now only one man remains."

"Ringleader," Thomas concluded.

"Yes."

Thomas leaned back in his chair, thumbing the rim of the cracked mug he held. "I want to be the one that kills him," he said. "I've thought of nothing else for years."

"It has to be you," Rella said. "The only reason he still lives is that he possesses a device forged for the purpose of disrupting living symbioids. A piece of symbioid is woven within it that has this power. I have tried many times … I have failed many times." Rella straightened and looked right at Thomas without blinking. "I need you to remove the only thing in this world that can stop me from achieving my goal."

Thomas winced. He remembered the golden orb that caused his father to writhe as Blink was torn from him. "Will this device affect my grapples, my symbioid?"

"Not enough to immobilise you," Rella replied. "They are 'only' mechanical; the orb affects conscious symbioids more."

"I feel as if I'm missing something," Thomas said. "You're not telling me the whole story. What is your goal?"

Rella gazed at Thomas with lifeless eyes, his animated features stilled. Thomas's ears prickled like he was in the wild and had just come face-to-face with a predator.

There was a knock at the door, and the two looked up as the zombie tending the fire shuffled over and opened it with disjointed motions. Two other zombies entered, carrying a trembling figure, the man Thomas had pursued into the zombie quarter. They threw him on the ground by the table and stood by.

"This one ready to speak," one of the zombies said in a rasping voice.

"Thank you," Rella said, his animated features returning as he moved to stand over the smuggler. He shot out an arm and grabbed the smuggler's jawline, jerking his head to look up at him. "Do you know who I am?" Rella asked calmly, sinisterly.

"Y-yes," the smuggler said.

"Have my scions explained to you what would happen should you refuse to answer my questions?" Rella said.

"Y-yes, please don't turn me into one of those things!"

"That depends entirely on you, human. Now, where is the one you are smuggling out of the city tonight?"

"I don't know where he is!" the smuggler cried. "I swear!"

Rella sighed. Then his face contorted as sinewy tendrils erupted from the skin of his hand and slithered over the face of the terrified man. Thomas sniffed, smelling fresh urine as the smuggler pissed himself.

"No, no, please!" he screamed.

"Then tell me what I want to know!" Rella roared.

"I can tell you where he is going to be!" the smuggler whimpered.

The tendrils froze in place and then slowly retracted back into Rella's hand.

"Go on."

"He's due to meet a ship in port to take him across the sea. He knows a path through the Buttress Quarter, which should lead him un-assaulted to the port. He'll be taking it tonight." The smuggler was panting, quivering. Sweat made his face shine.

Rella released his grip on the man, allowing him to crumple to the ground. "Excellent!" he said pleasantly. "Would you mind marking this path on a map?"

"N-not at all," the smuggler whimpered from the ground.

"How delightful!" Rella nodded to one of the zombies, who produced a folded sheet and quill with a bottle of ink. "Please, sit." Rella picked up the smuggler and pulled out a chair for him at the table.

The smuggler sat and unfolded the sheet with shaking hands to reveal a map of the city, and he traced a rough line through the Buttress Quarter, a path to the docks.

Rella studied the process while twirling the end of his moustache as Thomas sipped the last dreg of tea from the bottom of his shattered mug, seemingly invisible to the terrified hostage.

"Hmm, a smart path—Thomas, we should intercept him here." Rella pointed at a square on the map. "An open quadrangle with surrounding spires, ideal for a man with grappling hooks."

The smuggler noticed Thomas for the first time. "You?"

"Yes, me." Thomas rose from his chair, placing his empty, broken teacup on the table.

Rella picked up his hat, positioned his monocle on his eye, and spoke to the zombies in the room. "Keep this man here until tomorrow morning so that he does not warn our quarry. Then release him unharmed. Perhaps he would care for some tea?"

The zombies made no signs of registering his order, but Rella seemed satisfied they would obey.

"Well, then," he said, picking up his umbrella from a rack by the door. "Shall we be off, Thomas?"

"After you."

Rella pushed open the door and exited into the dimming day. Thomas glanced back one last time at the smuggler, who sat hunched over. He felt some measure of pity for the man, but he would be all right. He followed Rella outside.

The breeze was crisp, and it was a lot colder outside than inside, even with the collapsed roof. Rella was waiting, watching the sun as it dipped below the horizon, with a smile on his face.

"Soon, Thomas, soon things shall be put right, for you, and for me." He turned to the mercenary. "Shall we? I can take over your symbioid again to lead the way?"

"I would rather control myself, thank you very much," Thomas said.

"Very well, follow me!" Rella bounded across the street and leaped up the adjacent building like a leopard.

Thomas raised his grapples and fired, swinging after the zombie master.

#

It took little time to traverse the city to the Buttress Quarter, and even less time to find the quadrangle where they would set their trap. They both waited within the top of a spire for what seemed like hours.

Night had well and truly fallen, and the shattered moon spread out across the sky, casting an eerie pale green glow about the stone labyrinth, and the rest of the sky was alive with the dancing lights of stars.

"Hmm," Rella said.

"What is it?" Thomas asked.

"I can feel other symbioids approaching from several directions. Mechanical and conscious."

"Oh? Ringleader and his men?"

"No, I think he has not many symbioid woven agents left loyal to him … Be ready, should more bounty hunters and assassins arrive, we must move quickly to be first to slay him."

Thomas gazed down into the nightmarish shadows of the place, thinking hard. "Why not just let them kill him? I mean, I would prefer to be the one to kill him, but our vengeance is served either way … so long as he does not escape."

"Because I can't let anyone else get their hands on the orb he carries. It could be catastrophic to me if more symbioids are ripped from their hosts for nefarious purposes." Rella answered.

"Fair enough," Thomas conceded, but then another thought struck him. "Rella, why did Blink not stay with you—if it did indeed combine with the other symbioids to allow your creation?"

Rella's animated expressions stilled again, disquieting Thomas. "It disagreed with my purpose," he finally said.

"Isn't it you?" Thomas said, furrowing his brow.

Rella smiled again, the pale light casting his shadowed, moustached face into sinister form. "Have you not ever experienced turmoil within, Thomas?" His monocle flashed as he shot Thomas a glance.

"I guess … What is your purpose? The one that Blink disagreed with?"

Rella's smile vanished.

"Rella?"

"Something wicked this way comes," Rella said and slinked away.

Thomas was going to press him for answers but heard the tentative footsteps of someone entering the quadrangle. He glanced down, and his blood ran cold.

Eric …

His mind raced, piecing it all together.

His uncle needed protecting because he is the ringleader of the Symbicate, currently beset upon by numerous bounties and criminal organisations he had run out of favour with, by bounties placed by authorities who now had the information they needed on him to issue warrants for his arrest. The Blink was given to Eric by his uncle—by Ringleader—not as an inheritance, but as the spoils of war after ripping it from my father.

Did Eric know? Did he know his family destroyed mine and continue to treat me like a friend?

His rage peaked as the figure waiting in the shadows behind Eric shifted, an old man in a golden coat, the same man who had ripped the symbioid and ordered the murder of his father and sold his sister into slavery.

Thomas's teeth clenched, setting his face into an angry leer. He drew his blades with white-knuckled fists and fired his grapple to swing down.

"Viscount!" Thomas's voice boomed as he swooped down from his perch and landed in the shadows.

The ringleader stepped up behind Eric with a trembling voice. “I recognise that face,” he whimpered.

“Oh no.” Eric paled as the furious Thomas Marrow emerged from the shadows.

The two friends faced off against one another.

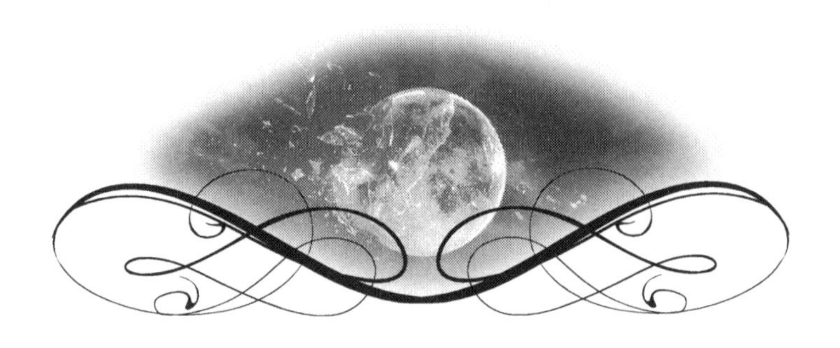

CHAPTER 16

All the Players

Thomas's face contorted with rage, with fury, and Eric knew why.

"Thomas, I . . ."

"Did you know, Eric?" Thomas's quivering voice echoed across the empty space. "Did you know that your family destroyed mine?"

"Not until today."

"That's cogrust!" Thomas stepped forward, readying his weapons. Eric raised his, surprised by his lack of hesitation.

"Don't make me fight you, Thomas," he said. "I won't lose a friend."

"Don't make me kill you, Eric." Thomas clenched his teeth. "I wouldn't want to filth my blade on swine."

"Thomas, please."

A scrape in the shadows of metal on stone. Eric's eyes flickered towards it in the dimness. Thomas's gaze remained fixated firmly through Eric, homing in on the ringleader, on Constantine.

Constantine grabbed Eric's shoulder. "Enough of this, nephew, we must flee."

"You shut your mouth!" Eric hissed.

"No," Thomas said. "Let him speak, let him justify his actions to me—the last surviving Marrow."

"Ah," Constantine's voice trembled, from fear instead of rage, "I thought I recognised you." He inched out around Eric, putting on a show of bravado that was all but washed away by heavy drops of sweat. "The Tinkerer's son, I thought you dead."

"I may as well have been. I have bent all of my efforts towards hunting you down." Thomas pointed with his sabre and stepped forward.

Eric stepped forward also, once again putting himself between the two.

"And how tragic, that you should bend all of your will just to die now. Do yourself a favour, *Tinkerer's son*, and walk away, continue your family's line, or I will have Eric here kill you."

Before Eric could speak, Thomas cut in. "So, you are worse than a pompous swine, Eric. You are just a pompous puppet, on the wrong side of my vengeance."

"Thomas," Eric said, "don't make me do this."

"Enough of this, Eric," Constantine barked. "Kill him and let us be off."

"Obey your master, *Viscount*. I'm sure it's for the greater good," Thomas challenged.

Eric sighed and raised his cutlass—he hesitated. The all but imperceptible footfalls of an assassin charged from the rear.

Eric reacted instinctively—grabbing his uncle and blinking away. An instant later, Tara's knife slashed through the empty space that once contained Constantine. Eric and Constantine stumbled to the side as Tara swore.

"Tara?" Thomas's jaw dropped. "What are you doing here?"

"Ow, my insides!" Constantine cried as the blink addled his constitution.

"Quiet, Uncle," Eric ordered, as he rounded on Tara. "What the hell are you doing here?"

Tara set her jaw and pulled her hood down lower over her face, and her fingers hesitated as she pulled her yellow scarf—the one Eric gifted her—over her mouth. "I'm a Night Assassin, and if that man," she gestured to the dazed Constantine, "dies by any hand other than my own, my life is forfeit."

"Then join me, Tara. Let's get Eric out of the way together, and your blade can be the one that ends that monster!" Thomas said.

Tara shot him a sorrowful look. "Is this the man you truly are, Thomas? A crazed creature bent on killing?"

"Says the assassin …" Thomas shot back.

Tara winced inwardly, but kept her outward resolve.

Eric chuckled, drawing their attention. "I should have let you drown in those icy waters, *Mercenary*. And then I should have let those pirates take you." He pointed to Tara. "Murderer!"

Tara rounded on Eric. "You harbour one of the most prolific criminals in the world and dare to judge me? *Was* it for the greater good, Eric?"

"Tara, he raised me." Eric's voice was almost a plea.

Tara suppressed another wince. "I'm here for family too. Should I fail, I'm to be killed. And the children on the streets of my home go without protection."

"Enough of this!" Thomas roared. "Join me, Tara, or stay out of my way!" He launched his grapple at Eric.

Eric blinked forward—appearing before Thomas—and head-butted him in the nose, hard. Thomas stumbled and swept his grapple around, tripping the feet out from the tiring Eric. As the two grappled for dominance in the ghastly lit square, Tara advanced on her target. He was still recovering from the blink, and he came to as she grabbed the cuff of his golden cloak and raised her knife to end him.

She hesitated.

From her vantage point, Billie swore, and moved in.

Tara steeled herself and struck—but Eric had gained enough of an upper hand in his duel to blink beside her. He elbowed her in the face, she stumbled off with a cry, and Eric turned to grab his uncle—that's when he saw the throwing star. Eric just had the time to swing his blade up; he deflected the star from its path to his heart, and it sliced his brow as it ricocheted up. He screamed in pain, shuffling backward from the prone form of his uncle. Before he could recover fully, the star thrower emerged from the shadows. She leaped into the air, black cloak billowing and goggles glinting sinisterly in the moonlight.

The new assassin slashed down with two short blades in a flurry of motion, which Eric could only fall back under—barely dodging or parrying each oncoming blow.

Thomas grappled up a spire and swooped over the melee. He ignored the shadowy fighter who emerged out of nowhere and sighted his target. He dropped down into a roll as Constantine stumbled towards the shadows, heading down an enclosed corridor on the side of the quadrangle—Thomas followed.

Tara found herself on her back, Billie and Eric battling beside her. She knew Billie would kill her if she hesitated again. She hopped up, grabbed her blades, and followed Thomas as he sped down a darkened corridor after her target.

Eric parried a straight thrust from the assassin, and she utilised her momentum, rolling under his riposte and coming up behind him. She whirled widely to slash at his back, but he blinked behind her. He clobbered the back of her head with his hilt, and with a grunt she fell forward. One of her goggle lenses cracked on the hard ground. Eric scanned the area desperately for his uncle as the tail end of Tara's leather jacket dashed into the shadows.

"Uncle!" He took off after her.

Before he had cleared the quadrangle, a newcomer entered from the adjacent corridor, a woman with dark brown skin. *A Baul Islander?* he wondered. She had a ridiculously large sword at the ready.

"Are you here to claim the bounty too?" she asked.

"Cogrust, more mercenaries?" Eric swore. "I don't have time for this!" He blinked down the darkened corridor.

Eleanor turned to pursue him when a voice caught her attention from the courtyard.

"You?" Billie dragged herself from the cobblestones. One of her lenses was cracked, but her goggles still whirred to zoom in on Eleanor's face.

"Billie …" Eleanor remembered her from the caravan. "Perhaps we were always going to come to blows."

"Perhaps …" Billie sighed, and with the speed of a striking snake, she flung two throwing stars in quick succession.

Eleanor activated the symbioid in her sword, and it fanned out to create a broad shield. She crouched behind it as the two projectiles pinged harmlessly off it. She hefted her shield and whirled it as she collapsed it back to a blade to strike, catching Billie off guard as the assassin rushed in—slashing her arm. Billie gasped, clutching the fresh cut on her arm, then dropped a smoke bomb, and rushed in to engage Eleanor in the disorientating smoke.

#

Luck, Luke Sill thought, *I love it, but it makes no sense.*

He whistled to himself as he wound his way through the labyrinth of the Buttress Quarter. The two serving girls he bedded had not given him access to the information broker, but had mentioned some strange goings-on about this part of town—so he just went wandering.

"Ah," he said as the clash of weapons echoed across the labyrinthine space. "How lucky." He grinned stupidly and took off down the next corridor.

#

Thomas bolted down the dark corridor and out into an opening that exploded with more ghastly moonlight. Constantine hadn't slowed down, his path taking him along the edge of a canal, and Thomas followed after him. As he was about to catch his quarry, a man burst out of an adjacent corridor. He was tall, pale, bald, and wore a long black military cloak. He barrelled into Thomas, knocking him off the edge and into the canal.

"Ooft, watch it, mate!" Luke Sill called down to him as he noticed the gold cloak heading around the next corner. "Oh hey, that must be the bounty!" He started after him.

A few paces later, he stopped in his tracks; another warrior emerged from another of the maze of corridors. He wore hastily patched-up banded leather armour and looked Estakan. He drew a long, single-edged curved sword and looked up at Luke from beneath his armoured conical hat.

"I here for Ringleader," he said.

"Well … tough," Luke replied. "Some good fortune will come along and distract you."

At that, Tara emerged from a tunnel and barrelled into the Estakan.

"Regen?" She gasped.

Luke turned as they broke out into a brawl. His luck symbioid never seemed to get tired, but this was the most consecutive lucky moments he had ever had. He didn't want to push it. He ran after the ringleader as a new figure blinked into existence before him. He was tired, sweaty, but armed.

"Cogrust!" Luke drew his own sword to fight the newcomer. "At least he's tired."

#

Thomas opened his eyes to the sounds of combat. He blinked the stars away, gazing up to the lip of the canal he had been tackled from. His body ached, but he was dry. He landed on a thin strip of stone which lined the murky waters beside him.

"Bastard blindsided me." He groaned, sat up, and aimed his grapple to re-join the fray.

There was the 'plop' of something surfacing from the water beside him. Arm still raised, he turned his head to see a miniature buoy bobbing along the surface. Thomas's eyes widened with recognition.

"Frogman, you son of a ..." He was cut off as a man emerged from the canal, clad in a sealed leather suit and bulbous helm with wide circular lenses fitted for his eyes.

He climbed up onto the lip of the canal. A cord separated from his helmet with a hiss and retracted into the canal, into the mini buoy bobbing on the surface, which sucked in and stored air, allowing Frogman to traverse the bottom of any body of water. He froze mid-climb, seeing the dazed Thomas before him.

"Hooks?" His voice was muffled; his surprised tone could have been that of one encountering an old friend unexpectedly on the street—even though they were bitter rivals.

"I'm afraid so ..."

The two looked at each other for a moment—then Frogman jettisoned two blades from his wrists which he caught with a practiced motion, and swiped at the dazed Hero. Thomas dodged backward and then threw his body against his half-emerged Rent-a-Saviour, tackling him back into the water. Now—Thomas's Hired Hero instincts told him that bringing an amphibious Rent-a-Saviour into the water was a poor tactical move. But he had unique knowledge of the man. When his snorkel was not attached to the buoy—a process which took several minutes for the symbioid to enact—he was as limited in the water as any other man, more so as his biggest fear was of drowning. An ironic weakness much like Thomas's biggest fear was of heights.

For that strange yet shared mesh of fears and methods, Thomas actually respected the man. But they were still rivals.

Thomas fired his grapple down into the depths of the canal and dragged himself and his unwilling companion to the bottom. Their battle dredged up the muck and filth of ages, and the already murky waters quickly became opaque. Their senses full of the pain of each other's blows, the feel of their limbs in each other's grasps, and the burning of their lungs.

Frogman's movements were becoming desperate.

#

Tara recoiled from another fierce exchange with Regen, the regenerating bounty hunter of legend. She clutched at a deep gash on her leg, but she had scored many more hits on him. His body was quickly repairing as the blood seeped down his clothes, his armour, and his skin.

She had the inkling of an idea, thinking back to when she had seen him skewered just a day ago. He relied more on his healing than on protecting himself.

"You should leave, girl. My target is not you," he said with broken words.

"I can't let you kill him; my life will be forfeit."

"It will forfeit here," he said. "I cannot be killed, but you can."

"So be it."

Tara launched forward, shifting past Regen's attack, manoeuvring behind him and stabbing him multiple times in the back before he roared and swung around at her. She rolled backward, his blade swinging clear overhead, and came up again at the ready—waiting patiently for him to heal, for the blood to become trapped outside of his body.

Over his shoulder, Eric was fighting the filthy hit man Luke Sill. He was losing thanks to poorly timed swings and bad footing, and the ringleader—Constantine—ducked back down another darkened corridor in the maze that was the Buttress Quarter. Behind her, the sounds of Billie fighting the Baul Islander grew closer as their battle rolled towards them.

Regen raised his blade, ready for another bout.

Tara attacked again, and again, and again. Every time she attacked, she was that much more out of breath, her attacks causing no ill effect to her opponent. Except for the growing pool of his blood at their feet.

"You not win," he said breathlessly. "I heal."

"Yes, you do. But not enough to weather a thousand cuts!"

She launched into an attack again, not going for the obvious killing blows that Regen was now protecting against under her onslaught. But she went for a cut to the leg here, a nick of the hand there—blood spray after blood spray.

Billie's duel with Eleanor spilled out of the mouth of the corridor behind her, with the Baul Islander switching her weapon from a sword to a fanning tower shield in order to control the flow of the battle. It was like some beautiful dance. Billie jumped and flipped and threw devices to break the impossible guard. But now they had entered the open, and the assassin could move more freely around her opponent's defences. Eleanor was on the back foot.

Regen swung a sluggish blow at Tara, and she caught it with one blade and stabbed him in the gut with her other.

With a grunt, he looked into her eyes, worry finally seeping through. "How?" he said. "I heal."

"You heal flesh quickly, yes." She ripped her blade from his gut, and a pitiful amount of blood spilled from the open wound, which closed over rapidly. "But you cannot keep up with the blood loss. I'd wager you have never fought someone more than a few seconds before your healing scared them off or allowed you to win."

"This is true," he said in resignation. "Very well, grant me my final honour, finish me."

Tara helped him onto the ground as the eclectic duels raged on either side of her. "No," she said gently. "I revered your stories during my training, sir, not because of your abilities, but your conduct. You would not take contracts that you thought immoral, you do not kill more than you have to, and you protected when you didn't need to. I respect you."

Regen looked up at her with distant eyes. "I only follow my honour."

"And you may live because of that. Now rest up, sir, and get some fluids in you once the battle has passed." She left him lying there and took stock of the situation.

Behind her, Eric slipped on a chipped paver and was clobbered in the face by Luke. He tried to blink around the hit man, who shot out his hand wildly and caught him by the neck as he reappeared. "Unlucky." Luke grinned. He clobbered Eric again with the hilt of his blade—knocking him down—and ran off after Constantine. Tara sprinted towards the nearest wall and leaped up it in a wall run, scrambling onto the rooftops, and took off in the vague direction of Constantine and Luke.

#

Within the opaque water of the canal, Frogman's movements started to slow. Thomas fired his grappling hook up and out of the water—and dragged his opponent with him. They sailed out of the filthy water and up onto the lip of the canal. Thomas landed with a thud as Tara scampered up a wall like a squirrel and took off across the rooftops. Eric struggled to rise from the ground, and an assassin was fighting a Baul Islander.

"Eleanor?" He recognised her from the Jaunt Saloon, as beautiful as ever. "What the hell is going on?" he mumbled.

Frogman coughed and sputtered beside him, and Thomas unlatched his bulbous helmet and tore it off to let him breathe.

"Why did you save me?" Frogman said between coughs.

He had pale skin and dark braided hair, which wrapped neatly around his head.

"Call it a professional courtesy," Thomas said. "I don't like you, Frogman, but I don't hate you. Stay here, and you won't get hurt."

"Yeah." Frogman rested his head on the hard ground. "Sure."

Confident that one more piece was off the board—Thomas grappled up onto the rooftop. Before running off, he drew a small blade and threw it at the assassin Eleanor was fighting. It glanced off the wall behind the assassin and caused distraction enough for Eleanor to knock her down and smash her boot against the ever-crumbing goggles she wore. Eleanor looked up to Thomas and nodded before he took off after Tara.

Billie recovered quickly, ripping half of her shattered goggles from her face and swinging her legs around into Eleanor's, tripping her up. They rolled into a vicious grappling match. While their battle raged, Eric watched as Thomas scurried out of sight and took a deep, shuddering breath before blinking up onto the rooftop, taking after the Hero.

#

Thomas swung across from a spire, nearly slipping in his wet boots. Tara was up ahead, and he knew that she must be zeroing in on Constantine.

Eric blinked in and shoulder charged him, and they both toppled onto the rooftop.

"Damn it, Thomas, let this go!" Eric shouted.

"He killed my family!"

Eric yelled in frustration as the two rose and stared each other down.

The shattered moon was descending over the horizon, casting sideways shadows amongst the many spires and buttresses that littered the rooftops. The east was brightening, promising a new day. A day which was too far away as far as Eric was concerned.

Thomas charged.

There was a gunshot, and a tile between them erupted into dust.

"Shit!" Thomas swore and ducked behind a spire.

"They'll need to reload, idiot," Eric said, advancing on the hiding Thomas.

Another tile next to Eric exploded with another accompanying gunshot and Eric himself swore—ducking behind a low-lying buttress connected to the spire Thomas hid behind.

"This is your first and last warning, Hooks!" a Soth voice called over the rooftops.

"Snipes?" Thomas said while catching his breath.

"I don't know why you are here, but stay away from my bounty!"

"Snipes, is that you?" Thomas called out.

"Who else would it be?"

"Snipes, I don't want the bounty! I just want to make sure he dies. You can claim the reward!"

"Now that is a lie if ever I heard one!" Snipes fired off two more rounds, causing the curious Eric to duck back behind cover. "You have had it out for me ever since that botched job in Foundton!"

"The tall spire, he's in the tall spire," Eric panted.

"Now," Snipes continued, "I've figured out that this man has TWO bounties! One for being Constantine Futruble for embezzlement and fraud, and another for being the ringleader of The Symbicate! There is no way I'm letting you anywhere near my payday!"

"Snipes, for fuck's sake! He's getting away!"

"Nowhere is too far for me, Hooks!" Snipes fired a few more rounds at their location.

"How can he fire so accurately?" Eric asked. "Does he have a long gun?"

"No, he has attachments which hone his blunderbuss," Thomas said through gritted teeth.

"How can he fire so quickly?"

"Another attachment, some kind of spring-loaded magazine set into a modified breach chamber, purely mechanical, no symbioid. He has maybe five shots left."

"We have to take him down," Eric said.

"Be my guest. As soon as you blink out, you are toast. All of those earlier shots were warning shots. He could shoot the precious locks off your head if he wanted."

"Look!" Eric said. "We might be at odds, but every second we're pinned down, my uncle either gets closer to dying or closer to getting away. It's in our best interests to work together."

"Cogrust!" Thomas hit the back of his head against the spire in frustration. "Fine!"

"What's our play, mercenary?"

"Oh, you're deferring to me?"

"You know this guy, I don't."

Thomas sighed. "Look, if you blink around fast enough, make him fire off the last of his shots, he'll need to reload. That'll take him some time and I can grapple over and take him out in close quarters."

"You think I'm some moon rock moron who'll act as bait on a whim? Why can't I just blink over there and fight him myself?" Eric asked. "I don't even need you."

"Okay, mister 'I wheeze after blinking once or twice,' you be my guest." Thomas glared at him.

Eric glared back. "Fine. Get ready."

"Once we're done with Snipes, Eric," Thomas said, "I'll fight you to get to your uncle."

"Understood ... Ready?"

"Ready."

Eric took a breath and blinked out into the open.

From within his roost atop the tallest spire, Snipes sat with steady arms, an unwavering eye aiming down the scope set into the barrel of his gun. He had solid ground beneath him, and a high vantage point. This was his battlefield save for one disadvantage. The ghastly light of the moon and the nightmare shadows of the Buttress Quarter made it difficult to sight his targets—but they were a twitchy pair, easy to spot when they shifted and moved. He had seen some ninja-looking lady slink across the rooftops moments ago, but he figured Hooks was the bigger threat. He was a persistent bastard.

Something appeared to the right—the teleporter with the fancy cloak. Snipes instinctively swivelled his gun and squeezed the trigger. The shot rang out in the spire roost—a dull crack compared to the trumpeted sound of a blunderbuss, a suppressed boom compared to the puncturing sound of a long gun—and hit the tiles behind his target. His target blinked and appeared on a higher rooftop, closer. Snipes reacted and fired. Sweat beading at his brow, counting his remaining shots.

From cover, Thomas counted with him. "Two, three, four . . . five!"

Thomas bolted from cover, steeling himself to dive out over the lip of a rooftop and into the air. He shot his grapple to a nearby spire and swung across the open space. He refused to look down at the rushing landscape below him, focusing on the spire, on the figure upon its top platform who was fumbling to reload.

"Snipes."

He fired his other grapple as he released his first one, and shot straight up into the sniper's roost, ramming into Snipes as he drew two revolver-fed pistols from his side holsters. With a wild swipe of his arm, Thomas battered the pistols aside, knocking them clear from the spire and down into the labyrinth below. Snipes brought up his rifle as a barrier between the two, but Thomas jabbed down over it, breaking Snipes's nose. Snipes slumped down onto his back, and Thomas wrenched the rifle from his grip. He raised the weapon high over his head and smashed it against the ground, again and again until it cracked and splintered.

He tossed the uselessly bent rifle onto Snipes's bewildered form. "Do I have to kill you?" Thomas asked.

Snipes shook his head. "But maybe one day I will kill you for damaging my gun."

"You'll make another one—until then, stay out of my way."

Thomas hopped up onto the railing, the thin divide between the spire platform and the empty space beyond. He suppressed a shudder—he could not let Snipes see his weakness—and searched for Eric.

He found him—alive—on a rooftop across the way. He was nursing a wound to his shoulder, bandaging it together with dressings he pulled from his cloak. Thomas looked over his shoulder at the dazed Snipes. “Nice shooting, Snipes.”

“Th-thanks?”

Thomas leaped from the spire.

#

Luke Sill found the ringleader on the other side of an open quadrangle yelling down an off-shoot corridor, holding a golden orb in his hands with menacing gestures.

“You better stay away, Rella!” he yelled into the darkness. “I’ll tear you right from your dead bloody host, I swear!”

Luke moved swiftly across the space between him and his target while he was distracted. There were continuous gunshots somewhere above, but he paid them no mind. Then two objects fell in front of him, and he tripped over them—faceplanting in the ground.

As he fell forward, a knife whirred overhead and embedded into the ground in front of him. “Cogrust!” Tara swore as she leaped down from the rooftops. She drew another throwing knife as she landed, but Luke Sill had already risen, and was brandishing the two pistols he had tripped over.

“Well, would you look at that!” he shouted, marvelling at the design. “Self-loading revolver-fed pistols; I knew I would get them, eventually. Now, this is a thing that *has* to catch on! Let’s test them out, ninja lady.” He looked over his shoulder to the quivering Constantine, whose gaze darted around the dark recesses of the buttresses. “I’ll be with you in a moment.” Luke aimed at Tara and fired several shots with each pistol. Tara ducked and rolled behind a pillar within the edge of the quadrangle. Luke laughed as he fired more shots at her position. "Come along, little lady, let's see how lucky you really are!"

Tara's eyes lit up. *Luck! His symbioid grants him good luck—perhaps that means it causes me to have bad luck at the same time?* Her thoughts were interrupted. Luke fired more shots towards her as he moved sideways, trying to get a better angle. She threw down a smoke bomb and relocated to another pillar. *Okay, Tara, bad luck. Let's go.* "I want to miss him," she whispered, twirling the throwing knife between her fingers. "I want to miss him." She made herself believe it; she *did* believe it; she didn't want to kill anyone. She took a breath and dove from cover as the smoke dissipated.

Luke Sill followed her path with his new guns and fired. The ground around her diving path erupted with bullet impacts as she threw her knife, aiming well above Luke's head.

The knife did not fly true.

Luke grunted, surprised more than anything. He looked down at the knife protruding from his chest as he let the guns clatter to the ground. Tara rose—the wind knocked out of her from her dive—and walked over to him as he fell to his knees.

"H-how?" he gasped.

"You are a vile man," Tara said, "but it still pained me to kill you. Your symbioid ensures that what is good luck for you means bad luck for me ... I thought it would be lucky to miss you and ease my conscience ... and now here you are—dying." She grabbed the knife and yanked it out.

Luke grunted again. Blood gushed from his wound—coloured oddly in the waning green moonlight—and he collapsed with a stifled laugh, dead.

Tara sighed heavily and looked over to Constantine, who stood there quivering. *Can I be this person?* she thought for the millionth time. *An intentional killer? This is different from the pirates. I sought this battle out.* Something within Luke shifted, and the sinewy, globular, and colourless form of the luck symbioid seeped out of his skin and curled towards her. "No, thank you, little one. I'm going to go do bad things ... find someone good. Go from this place and do good things," Tara said to it as she walked towards her target. "Plus, I can't stand the idea of weaving with one of you. No offence."

It moved with a squelch across the cobblestone, but Tara paid it no heed as she reached Constantine. She stood before him, and he held the golden orb up to her and activated it. Nothing happened.

"You are unwoven?" he whimpered.

She knocked the orb from his hands, and it went clattering across the quadrangle. "I am woven with death." She grabbed him by the cuff of his cloak again, and raised her knife to ram it through his heart. She gazed into his eyes—this horrible man who was now afraid—and was struck by the same thought that made her hesitate the first time, only different. There was a tingling down her spine this time, an instinct that compelled her to wait. *Am I really an assassin?* She held him there for what seemed an age. *Can I live with myself like this? The constant gnawing doubt that will one day get me killed? No, she sighed, I must protect the children a different way.* She released him from her grasp. "Just go. I will not sink to your level, not for any reason."

"Don't you know what you have done?" he gasped. "You disarmed me of the one thing that kept him at bay!"

"Kept who at bay?"

"Tara!" a shrill voice called.

Tara recognised it instantly. She turned as Billie—bruised and battered—emerged from the shadows. The luck symbioid was gone, nowhere to be seen.

"Can you not complete the task?" Billie asked.

Tara tightened her grip on her knives, pulled back her hood, and slid down her scarf, revealing herself to the world. "I can. But I will not."

Billie stepped forward, the remaining eyepiece of her goggles held in place by who knows what. "Tara, I'll give you one more chance." Her one exposed eye darted in confliction. "Our lives will be forfeit if you don't kill him …"

Her life will only be forfeit if she refuses to kill me … Tara realised. "Our lives already are forfeit, Billie. We are nothing but slaves to the Night Mother's sadistic will. I know you don't want to live like this."

"You don't know anything about me!" Billie was breathless, wounded, faltering.

"I know enough," Tara held her arms out in a gesture of peace, "but if I'm wrong, do what you came to do, kill me, then him."

Billie watched her for a long moment, and ultimately sagged. "You know I won't kill you. I could have killed for the Night Mother, but she had to go and have me train you. I can't," her voice cracked, "I just can't go on like this. Why couldn't you just kill him?"

"I'm not what she wanted me to be, Billie, and neither are you."

Billie grimaced. "So be it."

Tara stepped forward. "Billie … I …"

"Quiet! I've just sealed both of our fates. The Night Mother will not stop until we are both dead," Billie lamented.

"But we can fight her together."

Billie laughed. "You are so naïve, Tara. I guess I'll have to keep protecting you."

Their conversation was interrupted as Thomas grappled and swooped down from the rooftops above. He landed with a squelch, still wet from his dip into the canal.

Billie raised her blades, but Tara addressed him calmly. "So are you going to be Hooks, the vengeful?" she asked. "Or my friend?"

"Tara, don't get in my way. If you won't kill him then don't defend him," Thomas said.

"She has made her choice, *Hooks*," Billie said, stepping between Tara and Thomas.

She peered out from her black hood at Thomas, and her exposed eye flickered with recognition. But her thoughts were interrupted as another warrior entered from the far side—Eleanor, just as bruised and battered as Billie.

She glanced at Luke Sill's dead body, giving a satisfied nod. "I am here for the bounty on that man." She gestured to Constantine.

"Then I shall help you," Thomas said.

"None of you are touching him!" Eric blinked before his uncle, panting, bleeding, but sword at the ready.

"Eric," Thomas growled.

"You fools!" Constantine yelled. "We are all doomed unless we find my orb!"

"You mean the orb that ripped the Blink from my father?" Thomas spat.

Billie cocked her head, her jaw dropping.

"It's the only thing keeping Rella at bay!" Constantine said.

"Rella wants what I want. He wants you dead," Thomas said.

"I want you all dead!" Rella leaped down from the rooftops. "And now that the orb is gone, there is nothing stopping me from killing all of you!"

Tara felt a tingling in her nerves and shivered. As she shook her head, she saw something out of the corner of her eye: the golden orb across the quadrangle.

"Rella, what are you doing?" Thomas asked. "You said you only wanted those responsible?"

Rella's wicked laugh filled the quadrangle. "Oh, Thomas, you trusting fool. What I told you over tea was true," he shrugged in his unnatural, animated fashion, "mostly. But I am a creature not of your wretched guardian moon. I am the creature that was infecting it, fighting it, turning its sinews to one purpose, the death and preparation of all life to feed upon! You are all the same! And you will all die the same!"

"So when the Symbicate reconstructed the symbioid, they got you instead?" Thomas asked cautiously, the warriors fanning out around him in preparation for the coming fight.

"Oh, what a stroke of bad luck that was for them!" He laughed. "I nearly had your beloved blink in my grasp too, and now here it is, but first—" He leaped for Constantine.

Eric grabbed his uncle and blinked. They collapsed in an exhausted heap a safe distance away. Rella growled and turned on Thomas, leaping with ferocity. Billie and Eleanor rushed to help in the fight against Rella while Tara dashed for the orb. Rella took possession of Eleanor's symbioid with tendrils from his flesh, causing the sword to expand into a shield and contract back rapidly, shaking it from her hands. He then took control of Thomas's grapples, making them fire and wrap around him and Eleanor with the crushing strength of a python.

He turned to Billie and caused the symbioid in her remaining goggle to make her see all light as bright as the sun. She screamed and clutched at her broken goggles—half blind—and pulled them from her face, throwing them to the ground. One of her eyes was flared blind, but she could still see through one. She lunged at Rella, darting in and out with quick jabs, weaving around his odd, disjointed motions.

Tara grabbed the orb and shoved it in the folds of her coat and turned to the fray—Rella broke Billie's guard and kicked her in the gut. She went flying across the courtyard in a heap.

Tara charged, yelling a battle cry to get the monster's attention. Rella turned and bounded after the new threat. Tara continued unyielding towards the ferocious animal that was Rella. She knew he was a formidable fighter, but had gleaned an insight into his disjointed movement when he fought Billie. Billie trained her, and if Billie could land a hit, so could she, but she also had a weapon, the orb.

Rella shot his umbrella at her. It extended from his grasp and opened explosively, ramming her to the ground. He retracted it and leaped high into the air, whirling it around to bring the point to drive into her body. She dropped her last smoke bomb and rolled out of the way at the last instant. Rella stood in the haze, growling in frustration, searching for his prey. She ducked in towards the shadowy image of his form in the smoke and slashed at his face. He recoiled and slapped her down into the ground with the strength of a Baulsaw. He expanded his umbrella to an enormous size and flapped it open and closed, dissipating the smoke.

"A worthy human, but still food," he muttered. He crouched down to finish her off. She grabbed his bushy moustache from the ground, and pulled out the orb with her other hand.

"Fuck you and your moustache!" She punched the orb into Rella's face as she activated it.

It clicked open and latched onto his skin. A white light shone from it causing his whole body to writhe and vibrate as he screamed. He grabbed at it desperately, crushing the orb and Tara's hand both in his panicked haste to remove it, only digging it into his taut flesh.

Tara cried and recoiled, pulling her hand back, and felt another strange tingling sensation as Rella tore away from her, screaming the whole way as he bolted out of the quadrangle. His wailing echoed throughout the whole of the Buttress Quarter for minutes before subsiding. Without Rella's tendrils, Thomas's grapples slowly relaxed and unfurled, allowing him and Eleanor to become untangled.

"Are you okay?" he asked Eleanor.

"I'll have a limp for a few days, but I'll be okay." She smiled. "You?"

"I'll be right in a minute. Tara?" he yelled out to her prone form across the quadrangle. "You okay?"

She shot up her thumb, and then let her arm collapse against the ground.

She must be out for the count, he thought.

He glanced over to the assassin who had stood with Tara. She had the wind knocked out of her by the looks of it but seemed to be standing up on her own. Finally he looked to Eric, and the quivering form of his uncle.

"Now, where were we?" Thomas asked.

"Uncle, get to the boat," Eric groaned as he rose to face Thomas. "He's not going to stop. He's come too far."

Constantine scampered off without a word.

"A good man, that one." Thomas motioned to the scampering form as he retreated through another corridor.

"He had good intentions," Eric said. "You yourself sided with that monster Rella."

"I didn't know what he was … I still don't."

"And I didn't know what my uncle was!"

"But you know now! Give him up, let me have my justice!"

"It is not justice!" Eric gestured wildly. "This is madness!"

"Madness … in the name of the greater good?" Eric glared at Thomas. "This will be the end, Eric."

"If it must."

The two stood a ways from each other, sizing each other up. Tara, Billie, and Eleanor watched on helplessly, too wounded to intervene.

Thomas raised his grapple—Eric blinked.

Quick as lightning Thomas anticipated Eric's path and whirled to swing his blade towards his rear. But Eric blinked into existence above him. Thomas swore as Eric crashed down on top of him and pummelled the dazed Hero. Thomas shot out his grapple to the nearest wall and dragged the two combatants across the grating, cobbled ground, each trying to gain the advantage in the sliding brawl. They slammed into the wall, and Eric was knocked from Thomas, dropping his cutlass. Thomas managed to swipe down at him, but hit the ground as Eric blinked away in the nick of time.

Not wanting to wait for Eric to take the initiative, Thomas grappled upwards and swung across the courtyard, searching for his opponent to reappear. He saw a flash of motion on the lip of the roof overlooking the courtyard. Eric stumbled into existence, his fight wearing thin.

Thomas took advantage of his state and swung up to him; he landed deftly and side-kicked Eric off the edge. He fell to the ground below. Thomas looked over the edge—his heart catching in his throat—and breathed an odd sigh of relief when Eric blinked to the ground safely at the last moment. Thomas leaped down, eager to incapacitate the viscount quickly and continue on his hunt. He halted his fall with the aid of his grapple and landed heavily in front of the reeling Eric. He raised his leg to stomp him in the face—he would not get up from that for quite some time.

Tara rushed in before Thomas could land the stomping blow. Thomas turned and braced to defend himself, but she ducked to his blind side and ran up and along the wall behind him—one step, two steps, three—and twirled around with a savage jumping kick, clobbering Thomas in the face.

Thomas fell on his arse and rolled backward over his shoulder, coming up in a low crouch. "Bloody ninjas," he spat.

Eric shot up and moved on Thomas, but Tara was between them, putting pressure on his wounded shoulder to keep him at bay. "Enough!" she cried. "This has gone too far!"

"I can't stop, Tara," Eric said, drawing a knife in his good hand. "He won't stop until my uncle is dead."

He slashed at Tara's arm, and she recoiled. Eric lunged forward and blinked. Thomas anticipated his path and unspooled his grapples, creating a writhing web of sinewy cable before him. Eric appeared right before it, and Thomas closed the net. The cables snapped shut, tightening around Eric. The viscount tried to slash forward through the makeshift net, so Thomas spun him around and grabbed him from behind.

"Give it up, Eric, you're spent!" Thomas cried.

"I have one more blink in me!" Eric wheezed.

Eric blinked from Thomas's snare, appeared behind him, and grabbed him. He reached his arm around, trying to force his knife into Thomas's chest, through the visible gap in his copper plating. Thomas tried to grab at the knife arm, tried to force the tip away from his body, but his limbs were heavy with the weight of the night's exertions and Eric was using his good arm. The knife slowly forced its way between the copper plates beneath Thomas's maroon cloak.

The piercing sensation forced him to resist all the more and his mind to race, searching for an escape. There was none—unless. "Blink," Thomas growled.

"What?" Eric hissed through grinding teeth.

"Blink, it's me. I'm Bart's son, the son of your true woven host."

"What are you saying?" Eric said.

"You don't have to be with this one anymore. I'm family ..." He cried in pain as the knife sunk deeper into his flesh. "Blink, please! We can avenge my father. Together. Weave with me!"

"No!" Eric cried.

Thomas could not see what was happening, but he could feel it. The sinewy tendons of the Blink symbioid un-wove from Eric and into his own body, and he could feel the tingling sensation of its sinews mingling with his own. He felt the familiar warmth of his father's love, the conflicted love of Eric for his uncle, and the pain of loneliness—the same loneliness that Thomas had fought all of these years.

He smiled. "Welcome home, little one."

Thomas blinked out of Eric's grasp. Eric's knife—now without resistance—continued on its path, driving towards his own body, and pierced his chest. Eric gasped and fell backward. Thomas caught him in his arms, his eyes widening as he realised the full horror of what had happened.

"No!" Thomas cried. "No, no, no! I take it back, Eric, I take it all back!"

"Is this what you wanted, hero?" Eric said quietly, the life fading from his words.

"I didn't want this," Thomas said.

"Thomas!" Eric gasped, trying to wrench the knife from his chest.

Thomas placed his hand on Eric's, staying it. "Be calm. You will only bleed out if you pull that out."

Tara hobbled over, holding her hands over her mouth, crying.

"Thomas, please." Eric's eyes were growing distant. "I was wrong to fight you, but I didn't want you to kill my uncle. Don't become the man that killed your father. Do not allow the ends to justify any means, like I thought was right. Bring my uncle to justice, but please, let him live." He coughed blood, and his face looked pained. "Please, Thomas."

Thomas suppressed a sob, his voice shuddering as he spoke. "This is not what I wanted, Viscount. I will hunt your uncle, and I will bring him to justice … alive."

"I'm sorry," Eric said, his words rasping. "That it came to this." The life in his eyes faded. What was once bright was now dull and void. Eric Futruble was dead.

Thomas choked back a sob. His vision of Eric blurred as the tears filled his eyes. "I'm sorry too." He laid Eric down, placed his hand on his face, and closed his lifeless eyes. Thomas sat there for a while, and Tara came and sat by Eric's other side, crying freely.

"This has all turned into one big mess," she said.

"Yes." Thomas looked to the sky, which was brightening more with the coming dawn. "But the night has still not ended." He rose and turned to Eleanor and Billie. "I promised him I would spare his uncle, but I will still bring him to justice."

Eleanor watched on, speechless, then said, "I … I will help you, Thomas. You have just shown me what a life revenge and bitterness will bring. I will break from my mother's war."

Thomas raised his brow. Eleanor had reached some earth-shattering turning point in her life, but he had no idea what she was on about. He turned to the assassin. "And you?"

Billie stepped cautiously towards Thomas and Tara. "What is your real name, Hooks?" she asked.

"Thomas."

"Thomas Marrow?"

"Yes?"

She removed her hood, revealing her olive skin, pale from years in the shadows, and dark hair along with her bruised and scarred face. "I thought you died in the fire?"

"It can't be." Thomas's eyes widened.

"What?" Tara said, taking in her face. One of her eyes had scarred white in Rella's attack, but her other eye was a deep beautiful brown, just like Thomas's. Her hair was the same shade of brunette, and there was a familiar look to her face that Tara could now clearly see without the ever-present goggles on her face. "No," Tara gasped. "Billie is … Sybilla Marrow?"

"You were sold into slavery at such a young age. You should be dead," Thomas said, stepping forward tentatively. The night had caused so much sorrow that he was cautious of false hope.

"I was sold into the Night Mother's child spy ring, and grew to become one of her top assassins … I did what I had to, to survive. It seems you did the same."

Thomas stared at her, then rushed in. "My sister lives!" They embraced. "What a bittersweet night this is!" He broke down into sobs again, the catharsis washing over him, the fire that burned to avenge his sister washing away. Now all that remained was justice for their father.

They were interrupted by a cough. They turned to Eleanor. "I hate to interrupt this touching moment, but we still have a ringleader on the loose."

#

Constantine flew from the Buttress Quarter and into the bright morning sun. The docks were just a few blocks away. He had made it, and was safe.

A grapple fired.

His legs tripped from under him by the grapple cord, and he fell onto his face, hard. He struggled to rise, but something blinked before him.

"Eric?" he said, looking up to find Thomas.

"Your nephew is dead," Thomas said solemnly. "I am truly sorry." Thomas reached down and took Constantine by the throat.

"You took his blink? You aren't exhausted from its use?"

"I took *my* blink back. It is now with its true host and won't resist my use. It did take you quite some time to whittle down my father before you took it from him, after all."

"You killed my Eric!"

"You left him to die so you could save your own skin. His last words were still that of mercy towards you. I will honour his dying wish, despite the fact that you do not deserve it."

A crack of mirth broke through Constantine's visage of fear. "You mean to say that you'll let me go?"

"Not quite," Thomas said with a glare.

Footsteps behind, Constantine glanced over his shoulder to see Tara, Eleanor, and Sybilla circling around him.

"Constantine Futruble," Thomas said in an authoritative tone. "This is a citizen's arrest on behalf of the city of Masonville. You have committed crimes against human and symbioid kind alike, and you will face justice in Mason custody." Thomas punched Constantine in the face, knocking him out cold. "And that was for our father, you son of a bitch."

"I guess you couldn't just let him walk himself to the nearest station? Now we have to drag him," Tara said.

"Speaking of dragging …" Thomas detached the grapple guns from his wrists, exposing his burned flesh from when he was left in the burning workshop as a boy. It was an odd sensation as the dead symbioid withdrew from his skeletal system and into the mechanisms—like peeling off a Band-Aid from his soul. He offered them to Tara. "I have no need for these grapples with Blink. Would you like them?"

"Uh uh!" Tara said. "I hate the idea of symbioids, and you know it!"

"It is fortunate then," Eleanor said. "By my count, you took down three symbioid users by your own merit: Regen, Luke, and Rella ... and roughed up two more." She gestured to Thomas, implying her interruption of his duel with Eric. "You'd be far too overpowered with anything extra."

"Would you like them then?" He offered Sybilla the gauntlets.

"I would. Sadly my goggles are damaged beyond recognition, and the symbioid within needs to heal after Rella's attack. I tinkered with them myself, but I was never as good as Father. I will need a replacement edge in the meantime."

"Well, take them then. Keep in mind the symbioid needs time to fully weave into your skeleton for support, so no crazy swinging just yet. I tinkered them myself. Perhaps, together, we can fix your goggles?"

"I'd like that." Sybilla smiled.

"We'd need to stick together, anyway," Tara said. "To face the horde of assassins the Night Mother will send after us. I also need to get back home to help the street urchins."

"And we will have to contend with my mother's fury," Eleanor said. "She won't accept a split bounty ... And even though I won't fight in her army anymore, I still have my own mission to end the slavery of my people."

"These are noble quests," Thomas said, looking out to the rising sun. He laughed, thinking on how the people of Masonville revered such quests. "And Rella is still out there ... and more too." He looked up to the sky, to the last fragments of the moon as it sunk below the horizon. "We should form a new Symbicate, in honour of Eric, for the greater good, but only by greater means. We will form a Symbicate where we fight for the helpless and protect the world from more supernatural threats—like Rella and the people who broke the moon." He turned to the group—who exchanged glances with each other at his words—drew his sword—Eric's cutlass—and held it over the unconscious Constantine. "Are you with me?"

"Together," Tara said, drawing her blade and crossing it with his. "As soon as you explain that bit about the moon to us ... but we will prevent future falls like Eric's."

"Together," Eleanor said, crossing her massive sword-shield with their blades, "we will resist those who abuse their power."

"Together," Sybilla crossed her rapier with their weapons, "we will stop the vulnerable from being manipulated. And I will never be forced from your side again, brother."

Thomas smiled. "Let's use the bounty on the ringleader to fund our efforts. But first, let's get some much-needed food and rest."

"For the New Symbicate?" Tara mock cheered.

The group laughed and hoisted the old ringleader up and dragged him down the street. Hopeful at last that maybe there was good to look forward to in this chaotic world after all.

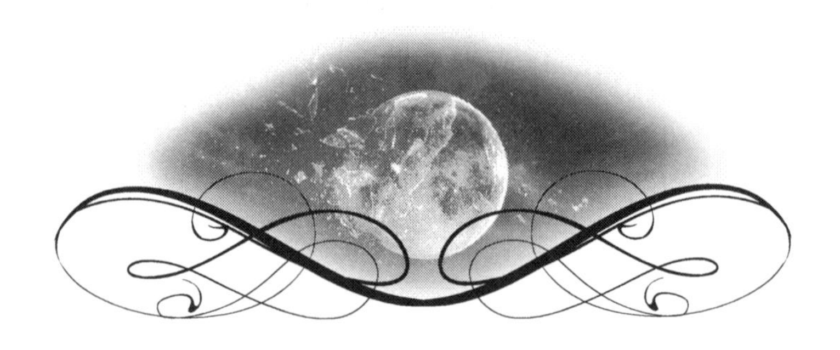

CHAPTER 17

Enemies New and Old

The jail door slid open with a creak that cried out desperately for maintenance, and the figure stepped over the guard who stopped gasping a moment ago, his fingers frozen in rigour mortis as they curled around the poison dart in his neck.

"Who goes there?" a tired voice called feebly from the darkened cell.

Sunlight streamed through the barred window in the hallway, and the figure stepped into it.

"Daniel." Constantine sat up in his cot; his gold cloak was filthy, his silver hair unkempt. "How long has it been?"

"It's been several weeks since, since we lost Eric, sir." Eric's butler stepped forward, pulling out a lock pick device from his coat which whirred and twisted by the use of external gears. "I'll have you out in a jiffy."

The butler inserted the device into the lock and waited patiently for the mechanism to do its thing. Constantine stood painstakingly and shuffled over to the bars, reached through, and put his hand on the butler's.

"No," he said.

"No?" The butler rose, staring down his master.

"I release you from your service. I'm done, Daniel. You should have seen the way Eric looked at me when he found out the truth."

"And then he died defending you," the butler said sternly. "I read the stories in the papers. A Hired Hero called Thomas Marrow killed our Eric! Don't you want revenge?"

"Aye, on the man who killed him ... me. Let me rot, good fellow. My final order to you. I belong here."

The butler removed the device and threw it at the wall. It shattered. "I want revenge! I loved that boy like he was my own!"

"And our way of life got him killed. Just ... just go."

The butler composed himself, flattening down his hair and adjusting his jacket. "Good day, sir."

"Good day, Daniel."

There was a cry of alarm as the Mason guards found their dead comrades. With a flash, the butler threw a device at the wall behind him, and it crumbled into dust. He spirited away before the area was swarming with guards, with a new problem on his mind.

For hours he wandered the streets of Masonville, letting the bustling passers-by knock into him, ignoring their raised fists and insults, drifting past the bazaar salesmen until he came to a barricade on an empty T-intersection.

A lone guard stood there, his long gun resting against his shoulder.

"Ho there, traveller." He raised a hand. "What is your business here?"

"What's yours, guard? We both know you can't fire that thing without a supporter."

The guard frowned. "This post is more ceremonial these days. I'm being disciplined."

"Why, is this not the zombie quarter? Should it not be manned adequately? I was here in the city when the incident happened all those years ago."

"Well, sir, the zombies left."

"They what?"

"Strange times, a few weeks back, they just upped and surged through the barricades to the closest city wall. Led by a screaming Rella if accounts were to be believed."

"Screaming?"

"Aye, headed straight for the abandoned quarry across the plains. Mayor would rather just keep them there. Hey, where are you going?"

"On a quest!" the butler called back.

#

It only took a week to cross the plains and track down the quarry in question; it was hemmed in by a Masonville stockade. The butler had little issue sneaking through. He bumbled past husks that growled at him but seemed too distracted to attack, and headed into the depths of the quarry, following the screams, following the direction that all the husks were gazing towards.

Before he braved the underground, he took one last view of the sky. The moon was scattered across the night in its pale green luminescence as always, but a faint streak of colour drifted out far beyond it, like a comet with a rainbow tail.

"Hmm," he hummed in thought, but he turned from the approaching streak of colour in the sky. He had more pressing matters to attend to.

It was dark inside, and the orange glow of his lantern did nothing to stifle the claustrophobic abyss that pressed in around him.

Then he found him, the writhing form of Rella.

"WHO GOES THERE?" he screeched.

"An ally."

"I have no allies!"

"I will remove the Symbicate orb."

Rella stopped writhing, and the butler loosened his bowtie as all of the husks slowly turned towards him. Like a pack of wolves eyeing a lamb.

"I'll just get a husk to do it!" Rella said.

The butler laughed. "It's been weeks with you in pain like this. It's obvious you can't."

"Name your price," Rella spat.

"Revenge, against Thomas Marrow."

Rella rose and stumbled up to the butler, buckling with every breath.

"I need a new body," Rella said through a wicked, pained leer. "My current host is too damaged."

"Then take mine. So long as I am coherent to see Thomas die, you can then kill your enemies at your leisure."

"Tara Night!" Rella screamed. "How can we find her?"

"I have some remaining contacts, some of whom would be very interested in hunting her with us … do we have a deal?"

Rella turned his cheek, presenting the embedded orb. The butler gripped it and wrenched it free. It was like a wave ran through the husks as they stumbled back. Dark sinew shot from the body of Rella and into the butler, who writhed and then stood erect as Rella's body dropped like a sack of bricks. A white moustache sprouted from the butler's face. He donned the monocle, the top hat, and took the umbrella from the dead host that was Rella, and then smashed the golden orb underfoot. The symbioid inside it writhed, and he stomped on it until it was mush.

"Hmm," Rella said.

"What?" the butler said with the same voice.

"It was smaller, that symbioid, than it should have been … No matter, let us go kill this New Symbicate you've tracked for me!"

A note from the author

Thanks for reading!

If you enjoyed this, please consider leaving a review. Leaving reviews is one of the best ways to support your favourite authors. The second best thing you can do is recommend their stuff to your friends!

My mission is to write kickass stories, with inspiring and relatable characters for all Sci-Fi and Fantasy readers to enjoy. I appreciate you coming along for the ride.

You can go to my website www.seanmts.com and head to the books tab to check out my available books as well as read regular free flash + serial fiction.

If you ever want to get in contact, you can email me: sean@seanmts.com

You can sign up to my mailing list through my website to get a FREE Sci-Fi novelette and stay up to date on my future releases.

You could also connect with me on social media.

Facebook: https://www.facebook.com/SeanMTShanahan

Instagram: https://www.instagram.com/seanmts/

Twitter: https://twitter.com/SeanMTS

I am always keen to answer questions, or just have yarn.

All the best, keep those gears un-jammed,

Sean M. T. Shanahan

About the Author

Sean works as a Tour Guide in Sydney, Australia. He has always enjoyed storytelling and considers himself to be a huge nerd, especially when it comes to Fantasy, Sci-Fi and History. The natural path from there was to combine those interests and write his own stories, which he started in 2015.

When he isn't scribbling down his whacky ideas or finding the worst pun in order to make his friends groan, he spends his time training in Parkour (in the hopes he will one day become an urban ninja).

Manufactured by Amazon.com.au
Sydney, New South Wales, Australia